I0728335

FIRST TO WAKE

NICKY PENTTILA

FIRST TO WAKE

SHAPES DRIFTED at the edge of Gina's mind like distant stars swallowed by twilight haze. Wet heat clung thick behind her eyelids.

She knew this moment. After a dozen years sealed in liquid sleep and chemical hush, she was waking up. They were finally here.

Gliese, their new home.

The long, flat rectangle of the sleeper ship *Autumn Dream* carried more than eight thousand hibernating souls toward humanity's newest outpost. Families and specialists committed to building a new life on a distant world. As the ship's lead medical officer, Gina would be the first to wake, to make sure the gradual revival process worked flawlessly for everyone else.

It was time!

She remembered the dimmed gray corridors, the four endless, cramped cradle rooms. Her footsteps tapping on the metal flooring as she walked through each room on final check. Walking the rows of celadon cradles—don't call them coffins—stacked two high, nearly kissing the too-low ceiling. Each one cradling a sleeping emigrant.

The growl of the giant box-octopus of a cradle controller grew into a roar as she neared the center of each room. Four whoosh-click tubes reached out for each cradle, three working and one backup. Frost like steam on the surfaces in the dry, chilly air.

Thousands sleeping, swaying gently in a nitrogen-soaked drowse. Must be the nitrogen compounds in the hibernation solution that gave the rooms just a whiff of a fish market.

She walked the foursquare of rooms backwards: Cradle Room Four, Three, and then a turn through the medical suite at the far end of the ship. Then Room Two, Room One, and back to the main medical suite, her suite, with its twenty-four small spa-like rooms for recovery.

Last in, first out. Gina took a final look through the window of her suite at the two thousand sleepers in Cradle Room One. All was well.

She'd stepped into her own cradle, and the mist pulled her down, into a long sleep she would have no memory of.

Twelve years ago.

But this waking up?

Nothing like the training video.

When a rush of warm fluid started pushing its way back up out of Gina's airways—as if her lungs had been drowning in honey—panic hit. She coughed hard, choking, a fat bubble escaping from deep in her chest as the fluid poured out in a warm, uneven rush. The bitter, oily tang of the sleep-soup coated her tongue.

She was upside down, naked, locked into place by padded arms reaching around her armpits, hips, and above her knees. Wherever the liquid that was now draining out was going, it wasn't landing on the floor, at least the square bit of gray-rubbered floor she could see through the small window. The reuptake drain must be toward the foot of the cradle.

A clunk, a hydraulic hiss, and the cradle started tipping up, going vertical, draining the sleep-soup out the bottom. "Relief water," three percent baby shampoo, started to cascade real and warm and loud down her dangling body. Maybe a little more forcefully than necessary.

Her breaths deepened in a series of gasp and sobs, now accompanied by the rinse-water thunder all around. When that quieted to a trickle, the padded arms holding her dropped away slowly, until her bare feet rested on the still-slick pod "floor."

What sounded like giant clothing snaps unsnapping were the six seals on the cradle unlatching, from head to toe. The front of the cradle opened like a door. Gina felt like a doll being unboxed. Then a real-girl shiver overtook her, shaking water out of her short curls and into her eyes.

The inset overhead lights were set to soft and

warm, like a holiday spa. But no one was waiting for her with a warm robe and slippers, much less a nice fruity drink. She squatted in the cradle, checked the distance to the rubbery floor, and, very carefully, slid a foot out. The floor was warm, and the air, too. She pushed herself the rest of the way out.

The square blue plastic recovery crates, one on top of the other, sat right where she'd left them, next to the cradle. Must have been a smooth trip. At more than a kilometer long, the *Dream* would have had to take any turns easy, even the mid-flight flip.

Gina used the gold chamois towel, and the wide brush, and—thank you, lord—the minty mouth rinse. Her clothes were in the lower crate: her favorite purple flannel tights, a sky-blue tunic that matched her eyes, big cream marshmallow of a sweater, and a sunshine-yellow headband to keep the curls away from her face.

She swallowed the mouth rinse, which held basic nutrients. It felt good going down and really did erase that bitter tang. Thinking of tomato soup and salty crackers, she slid her feet into cottony socks and then stomped them into the blocky black spacer boots. She grabbed her wrist communicator from the crate. Slipping it on, she smiled at the glittery eggplant of its stretchy band. The muscles of her mouth reacted a blink later than normal, which was normal.

So was the wobble in her ankles, and her knees, and her head. Best to try to keep standing, to wake up her balance and proprioception. Heart rate normal, respiration still a bit low.

She was alone in the suite, her sanctuary. Of course.

Three of the peach-colored walls held white-paneled cupboards with clear doors, stocked to the brim with blankets, towels, and many many rows of medical supplies. Every person on board had plastic crates like hers, neatly labeled and in storage. What they'd had on when before they went to sleep, and what they absolutely needed when they woke up. In the center of the long front wall, a doorway led to the hall of recovery rooms. The long back wall held sinks, freezers and coolers, and the window into Cradle Room One.

The window was clear, no frost from the rapid change in temperature in the medical suite. The architects had fretted about that for nothing. Through the window, the short, deep forest of hibernators slept on.

Everything looked good.

But something was wrong.

It was too quiet.

She tapped her wristcom. It glitched once, then twice, finally chirping faintly: Update needed. Of course. Twelve years of updates, probably.

That would take a while.

Gina staggered drunkenly toward the front of the room, into the deep pale-blue hall and its twelve parallel doorways that opened into to recovery rooms. She pushed the white door curtain aside to look into Waking Room One.

No cradle.

Where was the pilot?

And where was her team?

Not in Rooms Two, Three, or Four.

Gina swayed, holding the curtain to Room Four to help her keep her balance. Her thoughts were fuzzy, yes, but she was pretty sure getting the team up and active was Step Two on the list of Things to Do.

The defrosting took days. The ship should have already moved their cradles here. The process should have started.

Gina oriented herself, visualizing the ship's schematics she'd memorized during training. The medical suite where she stood formed a bridge between two worlds: behind her, the four vast cryo rooms. Across the wide hall corridor, a matching medical suite, with a view of Cradle Room Four. Everything redundant, just in case.

Her team wouldn't be there, would they?

Past the twin medical suites, the corridor led past a kitchen, a living and sleeping area that could accommodate sixteen, and then the navigation hub. The layout mirrored at the ship's center, which was the wall between Cradle Rooms One and Two and Rooms Three and Four. Matching medical suites, kitchen, living and sleeping areas, and backup navigation down there. No one was meant to stay on-ship long.

Even the medical teams didn't have quarters, just pull-down beds in the last two spa rooms.

The ship would glide through space on autopilot, its human cargo oblivious to the journey until the pilot was needed to confirm orbit around Gliese.

So, where was the pilot?

Gina staggered out into the hall between medical suites. Gray walls, gray floor and ceiling, minimal lighting, as if it were night. Dusty smell, like a radiator turned on for the first time in winter. Air flowing, lights humming. Everything in its own rhythm, unchanging.

A ghost town. Gina blinked slowly. Her thoughts ran like old honey, slow and thick.

Then she heard a voice.

CHAPTER
TWO

KETCH STRIPPED out of her outer thermals and dropped them on the floor. Why was it so blasted hot in here? She'd left the hall door open, for airflow, and now it got hotter? This job was a crock.

The ship's cockpit—"navigation center"—smelled like an old riverboat. A blend of recycled metal, warmed synth-leather, and memory of antiseptic. As Ketch slouched into the molded chair, its worn padding shifted, an aging ghost cradling her. The viewport, not even half the width of the cockpit's outer wall, was streaked with frost. And now smudged by her hands trying to clear the view. But at least she could partly see the sprawling asteroid belt beyond—a lazily chaotic sea of jagged stones pirouetting in slow-motion grace.

Just pray the scanners and nav didn't freeze up, too.

Glorified tug boat captain, that's what she was, at

least for this haul. This boat even looked like a barge, flat, long, and ugly. Three weeks to get this ship of ghosts through the boulders and then leave it go.

At least there was gravity. Thanks to the corpsicles needing something that needed gravity, she just bet.

Her fingers flicked idly over tacky knobs and scratched panels. Standard nav setup. Nothing going on. She'd been plowing through the latest Della Dow novel, but the alarm had reminded her it was time to call in.

Like that was even necessary.

"Deacon base. *Autumn Dream* here," she muttered into her comm channel, voice a dry rasp. She'd get some juice after this, maybe take a nap. "Everything nominal. Big bad rocks playing nice." Already they were too far away—and the ship's owners too cheap —to get a real-time response. But the owners wanted timed updates, because the contract said they could.

The hull sensors crooned low, their readings transmuted to sound. The dull groans and rude pops of pebbles too small to bother smoking pick-pocked her ship as if to test its boundaries. She heard the ragged lullaby of the impacts as background noise. Normal. Boring.

Threading a ship through buckshot asteroids had become her lonely labyrinth. A dreary physics puzzle she could solve now with eyes half-closed.

Good thing she'd brought her own entertainment. Owners had locked down the network to staff only. As if anyone would cruise out to this wreck to siphon entertainment or whatever secrets weirdo space colonists held.

Ketch had been born out here. She wouldn't have come out willingly.

Too many ghosts.

She was deep into Della Dow's very fictional jungle world—would Stacey outrun the ocelot?—when the shadows moved.

CHAPTER
THREE

GINA GRABBED for the chilly metal doorframe into the navigation station. Her wobbly legs had gotten her down the hall, past the kitchen, past the showers, past the closed doors to the living and sleeping areas, but that was it. Each step had been a negotiation with muscles that felt like they belonged to someone else, her feet hitting the deck plates with uncertain timing. Her heart rate was still elevated—not dangerously, her medical training assessed automatically, but enough to make her aware of each beat against her ribs. At least the door at the end of the long hall was open. She leaned a hip against the door frame, waiting for her breath to catch up with the rest of her, her body's systems slowly remembering how to work in concert.

The transition from the hallway's dim, utilitarian lighting to the navigation area's constellation of blinking consoles sent pinpricks of pain behind her eyes. After twelve years of darkness, even the soft glow felt like staring into searchlights. She squinted through the discomfort, letting her vision adjust gradually the way she'd taught patients recovering from ocular surgery—small exposures, gradual adaptation, don't force it. But this was worse than emerging from a dark room into daylight. This was emerging from chemical hibernation into a world that moved too fast and demanded too much.

This space was all new geometry, full of shapes and lines that didn't yet add up to meaning in her sluggish brain. Light spilled down in uneven bands from above, a staccato of cool blue-white squares interrupted by strips of faded amber. The room was triple the width of the corridor, but cluttered with slices of shadow that seemed to shift when she wasn't looking directly at them. Her depth perception was still off, making everything feel simultaneously too close and impossibly far away.

A broad, horseshoe-shaped console took much of the space, all dark grays: metal, cracked plastic, smudged glassy bits that reflected the dancing lights in nauseating patterns. Its edges and surfaces were scarred by countless fingernail-nicks and the scuff-marks left by generations of sleeves and boots—a palimpsest of human use that spoke of long watches and tense moments. The wear patterns were foreign to her, nothing like the clean, sterile surfaces of medical equipment where every mark was cleaned away between uses.

Bellied up to the inside of the horseshoe were two tall chairs with a short little console in between, facing the widest window Gina had ever seen. The chair on the left was taller than the other—extra headrest, apparently—upholstered in a dark, resilient synth-leather that reflected the pulsing console lights in sickly rainbows. The other chair was lighter, less worn, but no less intimidating. Both molded to fit taller, wider bodies than hers. Everything here was built for people who lived in this space, who belonged here. She felt like a child who'd wandered into the wrong room.

A holographic projection hovered between the seats over the little console, its blue-white glow making her eyes water. Beside it, a larger projection flickered and stabilized over the center of the horse-shoe console—wireframe representations of space that her medical training couldn't parse. Her brain kept trying to interpret the displays as vital signs, heartbeats and oxygen saturation, but the rhythms were all wrong.

Beyond the touch screens, keyboards and what looked like joysticks in the front half of the console, two-dimensional screens were inset at angles along the outer perimeter. Lines of green, blue, and amber scrolled past in patterns that meant nothing to her foggy mind—columns of unreadable data, cascading numbers that might as well have been hieroglyphs. There was a spinning wireframe of what had to be the ship overlaid with pulsing dots—hazards Gina could not yet name but that sent a chill down her spine anyway. All around, buttons clicked or blinked on and off, each following its own logic, creating a low, ceaseless mutter underneath the background hum of the ship's air systems. The cacophony was overwhelming after the sterile quiet of hibernation.

Her gaze drifted to the view beyond, and her stomach lurched. The viewport was grand but battered, a sweeping window streaked white with bands of frost, mottled with the gray fingerprints of hands that had tried, and failed, to rub the condensation away. Beyond, space itself unfurled—no longer the tidy black of pre-rendered navcharts from her training materials, but a tapestry mottled and alive with debris. An ocean of asteroids drifted beyond the glass like bones in ink, each rock a pale, silent spinner tracing a slow spiral through vacuum. Some of the asteroids glittered as they caught the lights from Autumn Dream's running lights, beautiful and terrible. Others, sullen and dark, revealed themselves only in the half-second after a larger chunk passed and sent them spinning in slow tides.

The sight made her dizzy, or maybe that was just the hibernation drugs still working their way out of her system. She'd expected to wake up in orbit around Gliese, to see the warm glow of their new sun and the welcoming blue-green marble of their destination. Instead, she was staring into an alien graveyard of stone and ice, debris from some ancient catastrophe spinning endlessly in the dark.

From where Gina stood—swayed, really, gripping the doorframe for stability—the person in the tall-backed pilot seat on the left looked to be sleeping. They certainly had bed hair, gray-blond tufts every which way that suggested either a recent nap or complete disregard for personal grooming. They'd had something like pizza for their last meal, and some of it must still be nearby, judging by the smell. The scent made her stomach clench with unexpected hunger—when had she last eaten real food? Her medical training catalogued the details automatically: young adult, healthy weight, no obvious signs of distress or injury.

But there was something wrong with the picture. The person had no recovery crates, the carefully labeled containers that should have held their pre-hibernation clothes and personal items. Their extra clothes—mostly gray-white, maintenance crew perhaps?—were just piled up there next to the chair in casual disarray. How had the ship woken them up without her protocols? How had they gotten here without going through the medical bay?

A mystery for later. Her brain felt like it was running through thick syrup, thoughts forming slowly and sometimes not connecting properly. The dark gray desk around the sleeping figure, all lights on and blinking in that incomprehensible rhythm, was what she'd come for.

It would have the answers to why she was awake.

But first, she had to catch her breath. Her respiratory rate was still below normal, her body remembering how to process oxygen after years of liquid breathing. She should've stopped at the kitchen; she'd passed it on the way. Her blood sugar was probably low, her electrolyte balance off. She needed sustenance. But she needed answers more, needed to understand why, because eight thousand people were depending on her when she could barely stand upright.

The person in the chair exploded out of it with a violence that made Gina's heart stutter. They spun so fast it made her already unstable vision blur and tilt. Hunching down, backing up to the console, they held their arms out, hands up, as if to block her attack.

The movement was pure adrenaline, fight-or-flight response in full display. Gina's medical training kicked in automatically, cataloguing symptoms: elevated heart rate visible in the rapid pulse at the throat, dilated pupils, defensive posturing. But her body's response was pure terror—muscles that were already unsteady going weak, her grip on the doorframe tightening until her knuckles went white.

Young skin, wild hair, wild eyes. The copper of their skin was marked on the bicep by the faint, worn ghost of adhesive from some recent medical patch— the kind used for extended-release medications or monitoring sensors. Gina's eyes were drawn to it automatically, trying to identify the type, the purpose. Recent enough to still show residue, but old enough for the skin underneath to have healed. What kind of treatment required that placement?

The plain black tank top already shone with honest sweat, the thick cargo pants wrinkled and stained from use. No jewelry except a battered earpiece, and a standard black-banded wrist communicator. No hint of the crisp, color-coded uniforms the Dream's crew wore in training videos, or the casual but coordinated look of the emigrants. No visible augmentation. Not even a tattoo.

No identification of any kind.

The absence of proper identification made Gina's medical instincts scream warnings. Everyone on the ship should be logged, tracked, accounted for. This person was a ghost in the system, and that meant contamination, protocol violation, possible danger to her patients.

"Who the hell are you?" the stranger growled. Unfamiliar accent, something that rolled rough and uneven—outer-belt, maybe, words shaped by different gravity and recycled air. Panicky but not quite afraid. Not the clipped diction of training films or the carefully modulated tones of ship's crew. The sound ricocheted off the consoles and made the whole nav center seem suddenly smaller, more dangerous.

"What," Gina rasped, biting down a cough as the words forced their way up her sore throat, "is wrong?"

It was the wrong question, she realized as soon as the words left her mouth. She should have been asking who they were, how they got here, why they were in the navigation center without authorization. But her medical training was stronger than her protocol training, and something about the person's posture, their defensive stance, suggested they were as confused and frightened as she was.

Her question echoed, soft and almost absurd among the mechanical burrs and environmental hums. An indicator beeped somewhere in the console's depths, a gentle but persistent metronome that seemed to count off the seconds of her confusion. The faint ozone smell from the controls now soured with panic-induced body odor—sharp and bitter, overlaying the greasy-crust aroma of whatever the stranger had been eating.

"You are!" the woman spat, flaring like a cornered animal. Her hands came up again in a block, but her eyes skittered all over Gina's body—taking in the pale skin, the unsteady posture, the medical bay clothes that probably screamed "just woke up from cryo" to anyone who knew the signs. "Where the hell did you come from?"

The woman took a hard, defiant stomp toward her, boots clunking on the deck. She set her arms on her narrow hips, sizing Gina up with the kind of quick, professional assessment that reminded Gina of security personnel or military. Pale, slow, unarmed. No threat.

But Gina felt like a threat to herself. Her legs were unreliable, her brain still foggy, her hands shaking with fine tremors that could be hibernation aftereffects or simple fear. She tried to shrink back, to blend in with the plain gray wall beside the door, but her legs—clumsy, rubbery, and untrustworthy—failed her. She lost her balance, muscle memory and proprioception still disconnected after years of chemical sleep.

Her knees buckled and her left hand snapped out, seeking purchase. The doorframe's familiar, worn grit bit into her palm—a rough-surfaced lifeline that felt real and solid in a world that still seemed to shift and blur around the edges. The muscles in her arms trembled with the effort of keeping herself upright, and she felt a moment of vertigo so intense it made her stomach lurch.

"Shit," the person said, and suddenly their voice was different—concerned rather than aggressive. In a rush, the strange pilot was on her, large hand clasping her arm as if to haul her up or steady her—Gina couldn't tell which. The skin-to-skin contact burned, warm and undeniably real after years of no human touch. "Corpsicle, gotta be," the stranger said, her tone lowering a notch, becoming almost gentle. "Get on over to the chair, here."

The pilot gave her a careful, steadying tug, as if wary of her fragility, and Gina's body obeyed despite her brain's protests. Her legs faltered forward, feet dragging across the slick plating with an embarrassing shuffling sound that felt out of tune with the busy blinking and chirps of the console. The pilot's hand was warm on her arm, callused and sure, leading her slowly toward the chairs with the practiced care of someone who'd dealt with unsteady people before.

"Easy does it," the pilot murmured, keeping her hand steady as Gina tried to remember how sitting actually worked. Her body felt disconnected, like she was operating a marionette with tangled strings.

The copilot's seat loomed before her—a dark burgundy-gray throne that looked designed for someone twice her size. The padded armrests were smoothed by years of wear, probably decades of pilots and navigators, and when she finally managed to lower herself into it, the seat shifted automatically, trying to shape itself to her contours. But its standard form had been built for taller, wider bodies; the seam of the cushioning pressed uncomfortably mid-back, and her knees barely cleared the seat edge. Even with her tiptoes touching the floor, she felt like a child playing dress-up in adult clothes.

The fabric was sturdy and warm against her back, with undertones of old sweat and something like cinnamon—maybe nutri-bar crumbs ground into the padding by generations of nervous snacking. The scent of human occupation, of people who lived and worked in this space rather than just visiting it.

With a soft whoosh, the pilot's hand fell away, leaving Gina feeling suddenly untethered. She exhaled, sudden and unsteady, surprised to realize she'd been holding her breath. The loss of human contact made the memories crash back—fluid pulsing down her throat, the panic of drowning in honey, the terrible moment of waking up alone when she should have had her team around her. She closed her eyes and forced her muscles to behave, making her fingers flex against the armrest's cool, nail-scuffed plastic, grounding herself in the tactile world of here and now.

As soon as her weight had settled into the padding, the pilot was gone, boot steps echoing down the hall with purpose and energy that made Gina feel even more fragile by comparison.

"Who else is up?" the pilot barked back to her from down the hall, her voice carrying easily in the confined space.

Gina didn't answer immediately. She opened her eyes and concentrated on the console in front of her, trying to make sense of the alien landscape of controls and displays. Monitors to the left glowed with rows and columns of mathematics, but not medical math. Navigation math. Stellar calculations. Her hibernation-fogged brain stuttered and failed to find meaning among the numbers, the symbols swimming in and out of focus.

She held her wristcom toward the controls, hoping the proximity sensors would identify her and grant access to the medical systems. But the comm was still updating, its tiny screen showing progress bars and system checks. She could call up a keyboard, type her name and codes manually, but her fingers felt thick and clumsy, disconnected from her intentions. Maybe in a minute, once the tremors stopped and her vision cleared.

She rested her head against the headrest and felt the chair lean farther back, responding to sensors she hadn't known were there. The position was actually comfortable, cradling her like the hibernation pod but without the claustrophobic press of the padded restraints. For a moment, she let herself relax, let the warm padding support her weight while her body remembered how to exist in normal gravity.

No time passed—or maybe hours passed, she couldn't tell. Her sense of temporal continuity was still scrambled, moments stretching and compressing without warning.

Past the window, the stars and stones wheeled in their eternal dance: silent, immense, uncaring. The soft pops and clicks she heard from the speakers must be sensor data translated to audio—like submarine sonar, maybe, or the kind of proximity alerts pilots used when navigating asteroid fields. The sounds were oddly soothing, a gentle percussion that seemed more organic than the harsh electronic beeping of medical equipment.

Suddenly, the pilot was back, dropping into the other chair with enough force to make it swivel half a circle in protest. Gina blinked, her time sense still skewed. When had her chair turned into a recliner? How long had she been drifting?

"Cat nap? Must be weird, using your muscles

again," the stranger said as Gina slowly leaned forward in the chair, trying to coax the thing back to a sitting position. The pilot's voice held a note of understanding, as if she'd seen this before.

"Didn't see anyone else, but found these." The pilot had a squeeze bulb liquid dispenser in each hand, the kind used for zero-g consumption but equally practical for people whose coordination wasn't quite back online yet. "O.J., or tomato bisque?"

The choice felt monumental to Gina's sluggish brain. Her stomach was empty but uncertain, her taste buds still deadened by hibernation chemicals. Tomato sounded warm, comforting, like the soup her mother used to make when she was sick. She pointed to the bisque, and the pilot handed it to her, passing through the smaller hologram as if the miniature Autumn Dream made of dots of light was nothing more than empty air.

The squeeze bulb was warm and familiar in her hands, its surface slightly tacky with use. But when she managed to get some of the soup into her mouth, it wasn't the rich, savory liquid she'd been hoping for. More like thin paste, with a metallic aftertaste that might have been the hibernation drugs or just the reality of processed space food. Sometimes it took hours for people's senses to come back online after a freeze, she reminded herself. Sometimes days. Sometimes the damage was permanent, taste and smell never quite returning to normal.

The pilot seemed to inhale the orange juice with

mechanical efficiency, draining the bulb in less than a minute. She dropped it into a recycle bag attached to the console between them with such economy of motion that a thought flashed through Gina's foggy mind: Had this person been awake the whole trip? It would explain the casual familiarity with the navigation center, the lack of recovery protocols, the absence of any hibernation aftereffects.

But that was impossible. The ship wasn't designed for long-term occupancy during transit. There were no living quarters, no real kitchen, no recreational facilities. Just emergency provisions and basic life support for the brief period when crew would be awake to handle arrival procedures.

Drifting lights within the hologram between them seemed to dance on the tiny Dream's hull, a miniature light show that made her eyes water. Gina watched as a spatter of green dots slid by the half-shaded schematic of the ship—each one representing something she couldn't identify. Navigation beacons, maybe. Sensor pings. Warnings or promises, information everywhere that she lacked the training to interpret.

Something about the pops and clicks from the speakers made the pilot start slightly. Her hand darted to her earpiece with the quick reflexes of someone accustomed to responding to audio cues, and she turned toward a screen on the main console, her movements fluid and confident. A muted click— fingernail on ceramic—and one of her screens changed to a real-time image of a section of the Dream's hull, gray metal scarred by tiny impacts.

She manipulated a joystick with practiced ease, zooming in on something Gina couldn't see. Every-thing about the pilot's posture spoke of competence, of someone who belonged in this environment in a way that Gina decidedly did not.

Every movement seemed to raise a faint cloud of old, lost smells: ozone from overworked electronics, oxidized rubber, faint scorched insulation. Gina let them flood her senses, hoping to crowd out the impending panic she could feel lurking at the periphery of her awareness. The familiar scents of medical antiseptic and recycled air seemed very far away.

"Just a passing shadow," the pilot said finally, relaxing back into her chair. She glanced over to the screens in front of Gina, which showed nothing but the standard sleep-screen display of colorful bands and gentle animations. "See you got the computer to talk to you."

"Not yet," Gina said, her voice still rough from hibernation. "My comm's updating."

The pilot had a nice laugh, low and genuine, from deep in her belly. "Computer's a bitch. Says I'm not crew. Gave her all my details, and heard locks slide into doors all the way down the hall." She glanced at Gina with something that might have been sympathy, then ran a hand zig-zag through her hair in a gesture of frustration. That explained the chaotic hairstyle. "You here to arrest me?"

Gina tried to laugh at the absurdity of it, and almost choked again on the lingering taste of artificial tomato. "Yeah, no. Medic. I unfreeze the, what? The corpsicles."

The pilot winced at her own terminology. She had a wide mouth, expressive and mobile, the kind of face that would be terrible at poker. "Sorry. Yeah, these ships always creep me out. Ketch," she said, giving the hand signal for she/her pronouns. "Belt transit. Asteroid belt, I mean. I'm a pilot, I mean." Her brows crashed down, frustrated with her own stumbling explanation.

"Gina," she signaled back, though the gesture felt clumsy and slow. "So we're in an asteroid belt." The statement felt strange in her mouth, disconnected from everything she'd expected. Her thoughts were coming easier now, but holding onto complex ideas still felt like trying to grasp water. "I don't remember Gliese being near any asteroids."

The silence stretched out between them, thick as the frost on the viewport. The only sound was the undercurrent of the ship—low, almost subsonic vibrations, a slow mechanical heartbeat that seemed to animate every object in the room. The glowing panels threw rippling blue and emerald highlights across Ketch's angular cheekbones and the bridge of her nose, making her look ethereal and strange. Gina tried to anchor herself by focusing on those shifting light patterns, the way they caught on Ketch's wild hair and made her skin glitter with perspiration.

How could Ketch be so warm when Gina was still fighting off the deep chill of hibernation? Even wrapped in her oversized sweater, she felt cold down to her bones, as if twelve years of chemical sleep had frozen something inside her that might never properly thaw.

"Gliese?" Ketch said, and something in her tone made Gina's stomach drop. "Sweetie, you're still four years from Gliese."

The words hit like physical blows, each one landing with an impact that made the room seem to tilt and spin. Four years? That didn't make any sense. The room seemed to shift around her, the blinking lights from the console suddenly too intense, the constant sounds overwhelming. The vibration in the floor plating seemed to travel up through her feet and into her chest, where her heart stuttered with confusion and growing alarm.

Four years. It was supposed to be twelve years of sleep, followed by arrival and the careful, methodical process of waking everyone up. Medical teams first, then essential personnel, then the general population in carefully managed waves. Not... whatever this was. Not waking up alone in the middle of nowhere with a stranger who wasn't supposed to exist.

Gina squinted at the bigger holographic display, trying to make sense of the three-dimensional map showing a cross-section of the space around them.

There didn't look to be any planets nearby, just the endless drift of rocky debris. Big rocks, sure, but none large enough to be habitable. And no suggestion of the warm, welcoming light of a star that could support life. Definitely not the familiar configuration of the Gliese system that she'd studied in preparation for their new home.

What was going on? Why was she awake? Why was she alone?

"So then, why am I awake?" Her voice came out small, uncertain, a thin thread barely audible above the ship's constant murmur. All her medical training, all her preparation for this moment, and she had no answers. Just questions that seemed to multiply faster than she could process them.

"You tell me," Ketch said, and there was something almost gentle in her voice now, as if she recognized the fragility of Gina's situation.

They caught each other's glances, and couldn't look away. This Ketch, with her warm golden eyes and competent hands, hadn't been the one to wake her. The ship's computer must have done it on its own, following some protocol that Gina didn't understand. It made sense, in a way—ship's AI responding to an emergency situation by activating the chief medical officer.

But nothing else seemed wrong. The ship was running smoothly, the life support systems humming along normally, the navigation apparently handling the asteroid field without difficulty. If there was no emergency, why was she awake?

The seat beneath Gina's hips continued to mold itself to her body, as if the ship wasn't quite sure how substantial she really was. She could feel microscopic shifts in pressure against the backs of her thighs—a faint tickling sensation, the low burr of servo motors making constant tiny adjustments. Her boots didn't quite touch the floor, leaving her feeling suspended and ungrounded. She curled her toes inside the thick socks, grateful for the sensation of terrycloth and the known friction of synthetic rubber against the deck plating. She pressed down, as if she could coax the seat—and herself—to feel anchored, real, solid.

"No emergencies?" she asked, though part of her was afraid of the answer.

Ketch shivered—actually shivered, despite the warmth that had her sweating—and broke eye contact. She waved at the console with its peaceful display of blues and greens. "Not that I know of."

With every breath, Gina tasted memory and adrenaline. Her lips still bore the ghost of tomato and mint, but now another flavor crept in: a flat bitterness from the recycled cabin air and a mineral tang that made her tongue prickle as though she'd bitten foil. She imagined she could taste the dust as much as smell it—the residue of decades of human occupation, rich with stories she'd never learn, mixed with sharper fragments of half-burned electronics and the metallic taste of recycled air that had been breathed too many times.

She kept her eyes away from the vista outside as much as possible, but every flicker of movement drew her gaze back to the window. Through the frost-streaked viewport, the asteroids slowly spun and glimmered, each one a shifting sculpture in the ship's running lights. Some stones drifted so close she could almost see the miniature craters on their pitted surfaces, ancient scars from countless collisions. Others reflected only as faint, fleeting phantoms in the darkness. Each celestial rock—massive, ancient, remorseless—threatened to pull her mind out of the room and into the kind of existential panic that she couldn't afford right now.

The navigation center gave off a palpable sense of being watched—by the universe itself, by the blinking panels with their inhuman intelligence, by the weight of histories pressed invisibly into every button and groove. And above it all, the anticipation of eight thousand souls still asleep, depending on her to figure out what was wrong and fix it.

But she didn't even know what was wrong yet.

Gina's wristcom trilled softly, the sound oddly tinny in the ship's atmosphere. Update complete. Finally. Maybe now she could get some answers, access the medical systems, figure out why she was awake and what she was supposed to do about it.

"You can turn all that beeping off, you know," Ketch said with a slight smile. "Save your sanity."

Gina had to smile back, a small pull at the corner of her mouth that felt oddly human after the inhuman experience of hibernation. "What? You update your comm so much that a single bar of music threatens your peace?"

Ketch cast her a knowing look, with just a hint of warmth that made the navigation center feel a little less alien. "Yeah, sure, and that's the only cheery bleep you got going."

Ketch was moving again, spinning her seat back to face the horseshoe console with a dancer's economy of motion. The chair gave a leathery protest, squeaking and hissing under the sudden movement. Ketch's scent—tart, honest, lived-in—cut into the airspace between them, making Gina suddenly, acutely aware of her own smell. The antiseptic cleanliness of the medical bay, the lingering chemical traces of hibernation, the nervous sweat of someone whose body was still learning how to regulate temperature properly. She shrank back into her oversized chair, longing for the clean anonymity of the medical bay and its sterilized predictability.

After she figured out what was going on.

After she figured out why eight thousand people were counting on her, and she was sitting in a pilot's chair with shaky hands and a head full of fog.

Then the wristcom started to shriek.

CHAPTER
FOUR

THE DOC'S wristcom caterwauled through the navigation center, slicing a new note of panic through all the low bass of ship and void. Ketch felt the little muscles in her jaw and neck contract, some animal response she could never shake. Tension shot from the base of her skull straight down her back, nerves synced to crisis.

That blaring digital wail echoed against the hard edges of the cockpit, ricocheting off battered metal, bouncing up and under the consoles, rattling loose a sour note of old spilled juice from some mess long left behind. It overwhelmed her scanner's gentle patter of pebble impacts. Not good.

Ketch pulled up the data view of the hull impact sensors—all well, for now—and then glanced at the doctor. Small and rigid in the co-pilot's seat, so insubstantial that squawk alone might push her straight out the window. Too pale, this Doc Gina, with her tiny mouth and button nose and auburn curls pushed back from her face with that sunbeam of a hairband. Even backlit by all the busy holo-glow, the doc seemed to fade right into the synth-leather cushions; she made the normal-sized chair look like a suit of armor meant for two. The woman was still shivering —fine tremors that made Ketch hyperaware of her own body heat, the way her tank top clung damp to her ribs, how the recycled air that felt stifling to her must feel arctic to someone just dragged from chemical sleep.

The hellish squawking didn't shut down until the doc waved her comm over the nav console. Bitch computer liked her, though. Stole three of Ketch's six big side-by-side monitor screens to show her stuff, interfaces blooming like flowers after rain. More cooperation than Ketch had gotten in two weeks of coaxing.

Lines of green and amber bloomed across the screens; the health data for what looked like everyone in the whole cryo bank. Corpsicles. Ketch's mouth went dry, tongue gone metallic.

The near screen had a lot of numbers—and a lot of red.

"What's it say?" Ketch asked, voice rougher than usual. The air tasted wrong, acrid with something scorched in the recycling matrix—or maybe that was just her imagination, her pilot's paranoia looking for problems where there weren't any yet. It turned the aftertaste of the orange juice bitter, coating her tongue like old copper.

The doc didn't answer, just kept zig-zagging her eyes, reading the data, scrolling up, reading more. That little movements—how she chewed her nail and then stopped, how she hunched toward the readout—were achingly familiar. The face of someone trying to outrun fear with math. Ketch had worn that expression herself, bent over fuel calculations when the numbers didn't add up, when the only choice was between bad and worse.

Unfair to make someone solve equations when they just woke up. Especially after near a decade asleep. Bitch computer should have handed the doc the answer already, but that was the thing about ship AI—smart enough to wake you up, too stupid to tell you why.

Doc Gina gasped. Her hand went to her throat.

"What?" Ketch couldn't keep the exasperation out of her voice. The scanner chimed a particularly resonant note—something larger than a pebble, but not worth worrying about. She'd learned to read the asteroid field like weather, and this was still calm seas.

Doc looked at Ketch, her wide, open face all bewildered panic.

"Everybody's running low on oxygen," she said. She put her palm on her forehead, as if she was the one overheated. "Ship's systems can't figure out why."

The words hit Ketch like a wrench to the solar plexus. Her own hand touched her throat. She knew what came after red oxygen numbers—had heard the stories from salvage crews, the lucky few who'd made it to escape pods. The timeline was longer than most people thought, but not long enough. Not nearly long enough for eight thousand people.

She pushed the thought away, hard. Not there yet.

"Everyone?" Ketch squinted to take in the flow of the main oxygen status readout. Doc Gina switched the data into line graph view. Trouble now, and a nosedive into the red soon. How soon? Ketch's fingertips beat an erratic rhythm on the nearest tactile pad, the textured surface familiar under her calloused skin.

"All the cradles," Doc Gina said, her voice round with disbelief. "All the people."

Not good. Ketch felt sweat prickle fresh along her hairline, the nav center's warmth suddenly oppressive. She'd been comfortable here for weeks, but now the air felt thick, used up. Which was ridiculous— their section had independent life support, with air, not whatever antifreeze the sleepers were breathing.

But knowing something and feeling it were different animals entirely.

"So you're just the first?" Ketch said. "To get… ah… thawed?"

Doc's face cleared, some of the panic receding in a burst of concentration. "Right. I'm first, and then we slowly roll through all the rest. Only—" She looked back at the screen with the red. "The ship hasn't brought anyone else to the waking rooms." She shivered again, pulling that marshmallow sweater tighter. "And nobody—nobody—should be up."

She looked so lost, like a kid who'd woken up in the wrong house. Ketch could see her trying to think, trying to push through whatever chemical mash was still in her brain from the long sleep. It reminded her of her own first time in deep space, that moment when you realized how small you were, how far from help.

"Well, shit," Ketch said, the words sticking to the roof of her mouth like cold grease. She watched Doc try to hold her composure as the facts crashed over her. The way her shoulders drew in, defensive, familiar. For a second, Doc's chest rose high and trembled, and Ketch felt an unexpected twist of protectiveness.

This wasn't her job, wasn't her ship, wasn't her problem. But something about Doc Gina—how much she cared about her people—made Ketch want to fix things anyway.

"Show me what you're seeing," Ketch said. "Tell the computer I'm a friend."

Doc blinked those long lashes at her, bemused. Then she nodded, decided. "Two heads are better," she said.

Ketch started the formal request for more access— the same dance she'd done with a dozen uncooperative ship systems over the years—so all Doc would have to do was approve it. The computer's response was immediate, portals opening in the interface that had been locked to her for days.

Typical. Kiss ass to one person with the right clearance and suddenly you were family.

Outside, the rocks kept spinning, untroubled. A soft thump echoed through her earbud—a distant impact, translated to sound by her scanner array. Different pitch than the usual pebbles, something with more iron content. She filed the information automatically, part of her always listening to the asteroid field's rhythm.

"How long does it take to thaw one of you guys?" she asked.

Doc was frowning at the numbers, her fingers dancing across the interface with growing confidence. "Quick, a day. Right, almost two days."

"What was it, for you?"

Doc's brows arched. She looked down, at her wristcom. Talked to it: "My recovery protocol? How long, in hours."

Her comm wasn't fancy, except for that freaky glitter purple wristband. But it did have a tiny screen. She looked at the screen, and then shook her wrist, as if trying to get it to shape up and act right. Then she looked at Ketch. The dark part of her eyes had gone wide.

"Emergency. Eighteen hours."

Well, shit. No wonder she was so lost. "Can't wonder you're so wobbly."

Doc looked back at the screen, with its dropping

oxygen levels bleeding air, her face settling into professional focus. "Here," she said. She pointed to a line that was all black. "Whatever happened, happened twenty-six hours ago."

Yesterday. Yet the ship hadn't thrown Ketch any warnings.

She was right here.

"And what has your mother-loving computer done about it?" Ketch growled. "Just sat and waited for you?"

On the next monitor over, she swiped out the long view of near space and brought up the repair logs— something she'd been locked out of until now. The interface responded quick, smooth and eager. A new set of screens opened: lines of diagnostic pings and bot requests, a ragged backlog of automated efforts to do something—anything—about the plummeting oxygen. Warnings lined up like dominoes, each spitting out loud, indignant "not my job" alerts as the ship's artificial stupidities collided.

"Woah," Ketch said. "I take it back."

The ship had run thousands of tests in the eight hours following the first freaky readings, and ever since. First sensors, then known weaknesses in the tubing. Then the machinery itself. Then, everything all over again. Like a dog chasing its tail, but with more desperation and less charm.

Then, one of the ship's cameras, on a spidery maintenance bot, went blank.

After that, it immediately fired up Doc Gina.

As she scanned through the logs, the buzzy air seemed to tighten around Ketch's face. The whole room suddenly felt twenty degrees hotter, though she knew that was impossible. She tugged at her tank top, unsticking it from the prickle of sweat in the small of her back. The lights overhead seemed harsher, sharper, throwing new shadows that hadn't been there before. Even the familiar sounds felt different—the air recyclers working a little too hard, the scanner's impact translations coming a little too loud.

Doc switched over to the log data. She was a fast reader, her eyes tracking the lines with the kind of hungry focus Ketch recognized from her own emergency troubleshooting.

"Let's find that camera," she said. Using the console's trackpad, she tapped the log-lines, calling up the details on the next screen over. Both their heads swiveled to that screen, now showing an image from another camera of the area around lost camera's last known location, somewhere in the ship's guts.

Looked like inside a swimming pool. Doc Gina leaned forward, squinting. Her hands fumbled with the touchpad, and the view blurred. She huffed, frustrated, and Ketch caught a whiff of mint and something medicinal. Probably whatever they'd used to rinse the sleep chemicals out of her system.

"What do you want?" Ketch said. "I'll do it."

"Zoom in." The doc pointed to the bottom corner of the pool. "Need to see the drain by the wall, there."

All Ketch could get was blur, too. The camera

wasn't designed for this kind of detail work, just basic monitoring.

"Too far away," she said. They both squinted at the image, leaning into each other's space without thinking about it. Ketch could feel the doc's body heat, cooler than her own, and smell that clean, antiseptic scent of the medical bay. "What's that lump, there?" Ketch said, centering the view on a black blur against the dark gray background.

"Part of the liquid breathing exchange system."

"People's air?"

"People's lives." Doc swallowed hard, a click in her throat. Too dry.

Ketch reached under her part of the console and opened the panel door to what pilots had nicknamed the snack box—a universal constant on every ship she'd flown. Emergency rebreathers took up the top shelf, their yellow casings bright against the gray metal; the bottom shelf had whatever else, most often a few past-sellby-date protein packets that tasted like cardboard but kept you alive and lots and lots of water. She pulled out a water bulb, its surface slightly warm from the console's heat.

She tossed the bulb to Gina, whose fingers closed on it belatedly, as though the motion had to be remembered rather than reflexive.

"Okay," Ketch said. "What do you want to do?"

Doc lifted the water bulb and squeezed hard, the motion clumsy but determined. She swallowed slow, her throat working hard.

"We need to zoom in on that blur," she said, her voice stronger now, more focused. "Get something in there so we can take a look at it. Ship thinks it's a blockage, so whatever we send to look needs to be big enough to clear it."

"One stopped drain and the whole thing falls apart?" Even hearing herself say it made Ketch want to spit. How could something this big, this expensive, be that fragile?

But that was the thing about space. It bred weak points, hid disasters in the cracks between redundant systems.

"It's not like that!" Doc's eyes flashed, real fire behind the hibernation haze. She pointed at the screen again. "This part of the system is sealed. Triple sealed. Nothing should have gotten in there. Nothing!" Then she deflated, sinking into the chair like air escaping a punctured hull. "But it is one of the only parts that does not have a redundancy."

"Triple sealed." Ketch squinted at the black blur again, her pilot's eye trying to parse shape from shadow. "Must be the lost bot, then. Picked a shit spot to fall to pieces."

For some reason, that idea made Doc Gina brighten, color returning to her pale cheeks. "You think that's all it is?" She lurched forward again, her curls actually bouncing, and then had to grab the edge of the console to fight the dizzies. "There must be another one of those in the system somewhere. They must be able to pick each other up, right?"

She tapped the pad, rolling through logs and lists with growing confidence, her fingers finding their rhythm on the interface. "There! The ship tried to move one into that pool—a footlong spidery one—but it's too big. It's trying to take four of its legs off."

Ketch leaned forward, scanning the schematics that had appeared alongside the camera feed. The bot's design was elegant in its simplicity, all function and no frills. "Nah, just drop the two back ones and that extra battery pack."

"Really?" Doc's eyes were clearer now, the hibernation fog starting to lift like morning mist. "Can you do that? Modify the spider bot remotely?"

Ketch swiped sweat off her forehead with the back of her hand and checked the asteroid field readouts on her near screen. That spray of midsize rocks was coming up in about forty minutes, their trajectories painted in gentle blue arcs across her display. No trouble, should just fly on by. Like everything else today, routine until it wasn't.

"No problem," she said.

Doc Gina made the connection to the bot, her clearance opening doors that had been locked to Ketch for two weeks. Then she handed control over to Ketch with a gesture that felt oddly intimate, like sharing the wheel of a groundcar.

Basic operations matrix. Nothing fancy, just good honest engineering. Ketch bypassed the standard protocols, watching the system throw up security flags like confetti. No wonder the ship's computer hadn't tried this—too many safeguards, too much bureaucracy built into every system. Sometimes you had to break a few rules to save a lives.

Twenty minutes later, the round-bodied spider bot had been reconfigured. Two legs removed, butt lost, balance redistributed, and a whole mess of warnings flashing on the maintenance console that Ketch ignored with the ease of someone who'd been ignoring ship computers for years. The bot looked frankly ridiculous now, like a mechanical crab that had lost a fight, but it would fit through that access hatch.

"Sending it in," she said.

The bot's camera feed bounced as it limped through the conduit connecting its own pool—nutrient soup slop—to the troubled pool. Air exchange. The phrase felt heavier now, weighted with eight thousand sleeping lives.

Doc Gina leaned forward, hands gripping the edge of the console, her knuckles white against the dark metal.

The screen went dark.

Gina gasped. Shuddered.

Then the bot's light clicked on, and they could see the conduit again, narrow walls gleaming with condensation.

"Door to the old pool must've shut," Ketch said, though her own voice sounded strangely high.

"Right, right." Gina, breathy, sounded like she was

trying to convince herself. "Of course. Can't pollute the pools."

As if on cue, a swarm of cleaner bots—little metal and ceramic ants filled with either cleaner or rinser—came into view, passing over the camera and, supposedly, over the bot itself. The routine maintenance continuing regardless of crisis, because that's what machines did. They followed their programming until something stopped them.

Light appeared at the end of the short tunnel. The new pool. With that impossibly narrow access hatch. Preventing unauthorized access, at the expense of emergency access.

Ketch held her breath, tasting metal and recycled air. If it got stuck now, they were done. Double the bot problems and who knew how much time to fix them. A day? Two? How long before red numbers became something worse?

The feed jittered and stalled. Gina started to rock, as if trying to send suggestions to the poor bot, her whole body tense with the effort of willing the machine forward.

Then the bot was in the pool.

Gina grabbed Ketch's hand and squeezed, but didn't take her eyes off the screen. The contact came outta nowhere—a shock of cool against Ketch's over-heated fingers, soft skin against her rough. A warm current race up her arm, something more than just surprise. When was the last time someone had touched her without wanting something—repairs, transport, passage through the belt? The doc's grip was stronger than she'd expected, desperate but not demanding, and for a second Ketch felt anchored, like they were the only two real things in a ship full of ghosts and shadows.

"There." Gina pointed to the dark mass at the bottom corner, her voice tight with excitement.

On the screen, they could see it clearly now: a maintenance bot, big as a horse, lights off, wedged against what must be a crucial valve. Dead weight in the wrong place at the wrong time.

"Okay, spidey, let's get it moved." Ketch sent the orders to the bot, her fingers finding the right commands automatically. Sometimes the old ways were the best ways—direct control, human judgment, none of the computer's endless second-guessing.

The little spider bot approached the blockage, studied the problem with mechanical patience, and then extended its remaining legs to attempt to shift the dead bot.

The dead bot didn't budge.

"Come on," Ketch muttered, jaw tight. She grabbed a handful of of her wild hair and squeezed, adding more static to the already-charged air around her. Her shirt clung to her back, and she could smell her own tension—salty, sharp sweat that had nothing to do with the nav center's warmth and everything to do with the growing certainty that this wasn't going to be simple.

Spidey tried again, repositioning for better leverage, its movements careful and methodical. Still nothing. The dead bot might as well have been welded in place.

"It's not strong enough," Gina said, hope draining from her voice like air from a punctured suit.

While the bot was repositioning itself yet again, an alarm blinked on the long-range scanner. The asteroid cluster was approaching, right on time—a routine navigation challenge that suddenly felt like the least of their problems. Ketch glanced at the feed where the spider bot was still struggling uselessly against the blockage, then back to the navigation display where peaceful blue trajectories traced their inevitable paths.

Well, shit.

CHAPTER
FIVE

GINA'S HEAD was clearing by the minute, the chemical fog of hibernation ebbing like a sticky-honey tide. The world around her was coming into sharper focus—the harsh angles of the navigation console, the way the holographic displays cast dancing shadows on the metal surfaces, the constant whisper of recycled air through the vents above. She could smell herself now, the lingering antiseptic scent of the medical bay mixing with nervous sweat and something metallic that might be the hibernation drugs working their way out of her system.

While Ketch turned to the navigation controls, muttering curses under her breath in that rough outer-belt accent, Gina couldn't take her eyes off the helper bot on the screen. The little spider-like machine was trying so hard and failing so completely, its remaining legs scrabbling against the massive bulk of the dead maintenance bot with single-minded determination. There was something heartbreaking about its persistence, the way it kept repositioning itself for better leverage that would never come.

"Something coming?" she asked Ketch, her voice sounding steadier than she felt.

"Asteroid cluster," Ketch said without looking away from her displays. Her tapping called up plots of possible trajectories that bloomed like deadly flowers across her screens. "Biggish. Shouldn't be a problem, but I want to keep eyes on it. Any change?" She glanced toward the screen showing the struggling bot.

The spider bot was still scrabbling uselessly against the bulk of the dead maintenance bot, its movements growing more frantic as its programming insisted it complete an impossible task. The blockage wasn't budging. Might as well have been welded to the drain grate.

"Guess the ship knew it wouldn't work this way," she said, the words bitter in her mouth.

"Tch," Ketch said with a dismissive click of her tongue. "Sure can't argue with the mother-loving computer." She went back to testing trajectories, her attention already shifting to the next problem, the next challenge to navigate.

Which left Gina alone with her problem.

Hers and eight thousand others.

The number hit her like a punch to the chest, stealing the breath from her lungs. Eight thousand twenty-one people were going to die on her watch.

Eight thousand twenty-one souls who had trusted her, trusted the ship, trusted the careful protocols that were supposed to keep them safe during their long journey to a new world.

Her heart seized, a painful stutter that made spots dance at the edges of her vision. She gasped, the sound harsh and desperate in the navigation center's controlled atmosphere. The yellow headband suddenly felt like a vise against her scalp, pressing inward with every pulse of blood through her temples. The cheerful color that had made her smile in the medical bay now seemed like a mockery, a child's toy in the face of approaching disaster.

Eight thousand voices roared in her ears—not real voices, but the weight of responsibility. The crushing awareness of lives depending on her when she had no idea how to save them.

She could see their faces in her mind, the dreaming faces she'd walked past during her final inspection. Parents. Children! Young people, ready for adventure. Old folks, ready to share all they knew. People who'd given up everything for the promise of a new beginning on Gliese.

Her breaths came fast and shallow, but she couldn't get enough air. The navigation center's atmosphere, which had felt warm and close before, now seemed thin and inadequate. Her hands went to ice, fingers tingling, vasoconstriction, while her face burned with heat. Extremities frozen and a chest that felt like it was on fire.

Everything blurred around the edges. The holographic displays becoming smears of blue and green light, the asteroid field outside the window turning into a kaleidoscope of spinning rock and shadow. No sound at all beyond the thunder rushing in her ears.

How could this have happened? She'd been so careful, so scrupulous in her preparations. Made her team check everything twice, even after the base had cleared them for launch. Every system, every protocol, every contingency they could think of. "Fussy," one of her team had said during the final inspections. "Thorough," another had replied, defending her attention to detail.

And now… this. All her careful planning, all her preparation, and she was sitting in a pilot's chair four years from their destination with no idea why she was awake or how to save anyone.

This wasn't her area of expertise. She hadn't checked these pools. Had left them to the experts, of course.

So where were they now?

The panic attack felt like drowning in air, like the hibernation fluid was back in her lungs, cutting off her oxygen supply. Her medical training catalogued the symptoms even as she experienced them—tachycardia, hyperventilation, peripheral vasoconstriction, tunnel vision. Textbook presentation of acute anxiety response.

But knowing what it was didn't make it any easier to breathe.

"Whoa." Ketch's voice came from very far away, cutting through the roar in her ears. Suddenly there was a hand on her wrist, warm and solid and real. A palm gentle on her back, pressing her forward and down."Easy breath. Easy."

The move—she recognized it as a treatment for dyspnea. Use "shortness of breath" instead, so your patients will know what you're talking about, echoed the voice of her first-year anatomy professor, a memory from a lifetime ago when medical school had seemed like the hardest thing she'd ever face.

Gina gasped out, forcing the stale air from her lungs. She sucked in a breath, but the air felt so thin, so inadequate. Like breathing through a straw. But Ketch's honest sweat, the lingering scent of old coffee, and something that might have been engine oil on her clothes, offered a ground. Helped her to the present moment.

She read her own symptoms with clinical detachment even as she lived them. Panic attack. Acute anxiety response triggered by overwhelming stress and responsibility.

Correct, said her professor's voice in her memory.

Gina forced her feet flat on the floor, sliding forward a bit in the oversized chair. The deck plating was solid beneath her boots, warmed by the ship's heating systems, a tangible reminder that she was here, now. Real.

Ketch's grip on her wrist tightened for a moment —a brief squeeze of reassurance—but loosened again when it was clear she wasn't going to fall. The forward position did make it easier to breathe, like always. The roaring in her ears faded to a manageable level, though it didn't go away entirely.

"You need meds?" Ketch asked, her voice loud and clear next to Gina's ear. The concern in her tone was unmistakable, cutting through her practical exterior.

Gina shook her head, not trusting her voice yet. "Panic," she finally whispered, the word barely audible. "Attack."

Silence for a moment.

And then Ketch laughed.

Actually laughed! The sound was deep and rich, coming from somewhere in her belly. Gina could feel it through the hand still resting on her back. The vibration was oddly comforting, a physical reminder that someone else was here, that she wasn't facing this alone.

"About damn time," Ketch said with what sounded almost like approval. "Started to think you were a dumb robot or something." The hand on her back started to move in warm circles, so soothing.

Gina let herself feel the warmth, the easy pressure of human contact. It had been so long since anyone had touched her with simple kindness, without wanting something medical or professional in return. The circular motion was hypnotic, helping to slow her racing heart and calm the chaos in her mind.

"You know," Ketch said conversationally, as if they

were discussing the weather rather than floundering in the middle of a crisis, "this is a damn nightmare."

A laugh bubbled up from somewhere deep in Gina's chest, though it came out as more of a gasping hiccup. "Always happens," she managed to say, her voice still shaky but stronger than before. "The panic. But usually after the emergency."

"Guess that's good, for doctors," Ketch said, understanding flickering in her gold-flecked eyes. She set her hand on the front of Gina's shoulder and eased her up to sitting, the movement gentle but sure. Then she knelt beside Gina's chair like a knight pledging fealty, her weathered cargo pants protesting softly. She scanned Gina's face quickly, taking in every detail —the color returning to her cheeks, the steadying of her breathing. The way her pupils were returning to normal size, she hoped. It was the kind of thorough assessment that reminded Gina of her own medical training, but applied with a pilot's practical eye. "Must be hell on the spouse, though."

Wasn't that the truth. The number of relationships that hadn't survived Gina's medical career, the partners who couldn't understand why she fell apart after the crisis instead of during it, why she needed to process the trauma when everyone else thought she should be celebrating the successful outcome.

Ketch reached up with surprisingly gentle fingers and pushed the damp hair off Gina's forehead. The touch was cool against her overheated skin. With her other hand, she slid the yellow headband back into place, the gesture so tender that it made Gina's throat go soft. The concern in Ketch's face made her features glow in the console's soft light, transforming her from a stranger into something like a guardian angel.

Okay, so still a little woozy.

"Gotta get back to my rocks," Ketch said, though she didn't move away immediately. "Want a protein bar? Salty chips?"

"Water," Gina said, surprised by how much better her voice sounded. The panic was receding, leaving behind the familiar hollow feeling that always followed an attack.

Ketch reached somewhere under the console and produced another bulb of water, the surface slightly warm. As she stood, she wiped her hands on her pants, leaving a shiny spot on the black fabric that caught the light from the displays. She shook her head, setting the gray hurricane of her hair to sway around her face like a storm cloud, and Gina caught a whiff of whatever shampoo she used—something practical and unscented that smelled like clean efficiency.

Then Ketch threw herself into her pilot's chair, the leathery fabric squeaking in protest as she pivoted back to her screens. She started scanning the void again with the kind of intense focus you could feel across the room, her whole body language shifting into professional mode. Gina, who'd had to work hard over the years to hone her own powers of concentration, felt a pang of envy at how easily Ketch could compartmentalize, how she could switch from offering comfort to navigating deadly asteroid fields without missing a beat.

The water was good—room temperature felt like a welcome chill against her overheated throat and washed away the lingering bitterness in her mouth. She could feel it settling in her empty stomach, reminding her that she hadn't eaten anything substantial since waking up. But the immediate crisis still loomed, casting its shadow over everything else.

She needed help. Real help. From people who understood these systems better than she did.

She pulled up the short list of people on board who had been designated as ship's crew, their names and qualifications appearing on her screen in neat, organized rows. There had to be an engineer she could wake, someone with the technical expertise to solve problems that were beyond her medical train-ing. That's why the ship had woken her up—so she could coordinate the response, get the right people involved, manage the crisis the way she'd been trained to do.

Chief Engineer Morales, Section Lead Chen, Main-tenance Supervisor Diallo. All sleeping peacefully in their celadon cradles, unaware that their expertise was desperately needed. The medical files were right there—Chen and Diallo had no contraindications for fast revival, their bodies young and healthy enough to handle the stress of emergency awakening. But Morales's ALS risk markers meant she needed to come out slow, the careful process taking days rather than hours.

Days they didn't have.

Or maybe they did.

Gina turned back to the event logs, her fingers moving with growing confidence across the interface as her mind cleared. She tried to estimate how much time they had until the oxygen levels reached critical thresholds, but the projections looked grim no matter how she calculated them. The red numbers seemed to pulse with malevolent life, counting down to disaster with mechanical precision.

She asked the computer for an exact measurement, and in the corner of the screen that showed the image of the pool—where poor, sad spider bot was still trying its mechanical best—the ship obligingly put up a countdown box.

4:17

Gina gasped. The numbers were already counting down as she watched, seconds ticking away with the steady rhythm of a funeral drum.

"Four days?" Ketch asked, glancing over from her navigation displays where colorful trajectory lines now in orange painted the path of the approaching asteroid cluster.

Gina doublechecked. Yeah, no.

"Four hours."

The words hung in the air between them like a death sentence.

Too soon. Far, far too soon to wake up the engineers, to implement any kind of complex solution, to do anything but watch the countdown tick inexorably toward zero.

Gina's mind conjured images of the rows of hibernating emigrants floating in their quiet, safe pods, oblivious to the approaching disaster. Families who'd sold everything they owned for passage to Gliese, children who would never see their new home, older couples who'd spent their life savings on the promise of a peaceful retirement under alien suns. Scientists and farmers, engineers and teachers, all of them trusting that the ship would carry them safely to their destination.

She couldn't even wake people up to warn them. The sleepers breathed the viscous hibernation fluid for nearly the entire recovery time, their lungs slowly learning to process air again as the chemicals cleared from their systems. She'd retched out the last of it only moments before she'd awakened, and even then the transition had been violent and disorienting.

And where would she put all of them if she could wake them? The ship wasn't designed for conscious passengers. Nowhere near enough living space, kitchens, beds for eight thousand people to exist in a wakeful state. And what would they all eat? The food they needed for the first year on-planet?

Gina felt the panic start to swell again from somewhere deep in her gut, an icy wash of terror that threatened to drag her under. The navigation center seemed to contract around her, the walls pressing in, the recycled air growing thin and inadequate. She could taste copper in her mouth, feel her heart starting to race again.

Focus. She had to focus.

Next to her, Ketch was scanning the three-dimensional display between them, the ship and the space nearby. Her thick-fingered hands moved with practiced confidence across the controls, her weathered features lit by the soft glow of the holographic projections. But she was frowning as she studied the data.

"There's new stuff in here," she said. "Not on my charts."

Not something else. Please, not something else on top of everything that was already going wrong.

"Dangerous?" Gina asked, though she wasn't sure she wanted to hear the answer.

"Nah." Ketch shook her head, though she didn't look away from her displays. "But I want to keep track of it until it turns." She looked over at Gina, her gaze flicking briefly to the countdown clock with its relentlessly decreasing numbers. "Two hours or so."

Two hours until this asteroid cluster passed them. By then, they'd already be halfway to critical oxygen levels, past the point where any conventional solution could save them.

Gina stared at the screen showing the broken maintenance bot wedged against the grate like a sleeping giant, the beyond-agitated spider bot still trying to move that immovable object. The little guy's artificial intelligence was trapped in a loop, unable to accept that its programming was inadequate for the task at hand. It would keep trying until its power ran out or something stopped it.

The solution was obvious, and terrifying.

Someone needed to go into that pool.

Someone human, with the judgment to assess the situation and the physical capability to move the blockage. Someone willing to break the triple seals and enter a pool of liquid that was never meant to hold a living person. Someone expendable enough that losing them wouldn't doom the other eight thousand souls aboard the ship.

Someone like her.

CHAPTER
SIX

"ARE YOU A GOOD SWIMMER?" Doc Gina asked Ketch.

Oh god, no.

The question hit Ketch like a wrench to the gut, bringing up memories she'd spent years burying. Cold water, gasping lungs, the weight of a sinking ship dragging her down into black depths. She could still taste the blood-metal fear, still feel the burn of liquid in her airways. Swimming was something people did for fun on planets with beaches and sunshine. In space, water meant death—hull breaches, flooded compartments, life support failures that left you drowning in recycled condensation.

Ketch lifted her gaze from the holographic asteroid field to glance at Gina. Still pale as recycled protein paste, still shivering despite the navigation center's warmth, still buried in that bulky, badly knitted sweater that made her look like a child playing dress-up. The yellow headband had slipped again, pushed askew by nervous fingers, and her auburn curls were starting to escape in all directions. She looked like she'd blow away in a strong breeze, let alone survive a dive into a maintenance pool filled with liquid that could kill you six different ways.

Then Ketch looked at the liquid air pool on Gina's monitor, and her stomach clenched. The image was stark and unforgiving—dark water, almost no light, the massive bulk of the dead maintenance bot wedged against the drain like a sleeping monster. Black ice.

"It's a glacial lake, that pool," she said.

The words came out rougher than she'd intended, carrying the weight of old trauma and fresh terror.

"There's no other way." Gina didn't look at her, just stared at the screen with its two dumb bots and no good answer. Her voice had taken on the flat, professional tone that people used when they were delivering bad news. Clinical detachment in the face of impossible choices.

Ketch's eyes darted to the countdown timer in the corner of the screen: 3:42 and falling. Each second that passed was another step closer to disaster, another moment stolen from all those cryo-ed folks who had no idea their lives hung in the balance.

"Do we even have a diving suit?"

It was a desperate grasp at alternatives, and they both knew it. The ship's emergency equipment was designed for space walks and atmospheric breaches, not underwater salvage operations in toxic industrial pools. Ketch's own EVA suit was rated for vacuum and radiation, not liquid immersion. The seals might hold, might keep the poisonous cocktail of chemicals and recycled organics from seeping in, but "might" wasn't good enough when you were talking about drowning in industrial soup.

"Spacer suit would hold." Gina scowled at the screen, her small hands clenched into fists on the armrests of her oversized chair. "Right?"

Shit, she was right. She looked down at her own EVA suit lying on the floor close at hand—gray and black composite material designed to keep the void out, environmental seals rated for extreme conditions. It would hold against liquid just as well as vacuum, at least for a while.

The suit was standard issue, nothing fancy, but it had kept her alive through more emergencies than she cared to count. She could see the scuff marks on the torso where debris had scraped against her during a particularly hairy asteroid-dodging maneuver six months ago. The left glove was newer than the right, replaced after a seal failure that had nearly cost her two fingers. It wasn't pretty, but it was reliable.

Yeah, no.

The thought of sealing herself inside that suit and dropping into that molasses water made her hands shake, her her heart rate spike. She tugged her tank top down as sweat broke out on the top of her chest.

"But we're covered in bad pollutants!" she said. "We'll poison the well."

Another desperate plea to find an alternative, any alternative, to what they both knew had to happen. The human body carried countless contaminants—skin oils, bacteria, chemical residues from food and air and the countless synthetic materials that made space life possible. Introducing any of that into a sealed life support system could trigger cascading failures, poison the very air they were trying to save.

"It's a risk," Gina admitted. "Also a risk to break the seals." She looked down at her hands, watching them twist together in her lap—a nervous gesture that reminded Ketch of birds' wings, fluttering and fragile.

And then she looked up, fixing Ketch with a glare. Daring her to say no. "I'll run myself through the decontamination cycle first. Twice. Better a little bit of bad air than no air at all."

The decontamination cycle. Ketch knew what that meant—chemical showers that would strip the skin raw, UV bombardment that felt like being flayed alive. It was designed for equipment, not people, though emergency protocols allowed for human use in extreme circumstances. The kind of circumstances where a little chemical burns were preferable to everyone dying.

"You?" The word came out harsher than Ketch intended, but the idea was absurd. The girl just woke up. She couldn't even walk down the hall without stumbling, could barely sit upright in a chair designed for people half again her size. The thought of her navigating a gigantic maintenance pool, working underwater with equipment that could crush her if she made one wrong move—with enough liquid that that itself could crush her— was terrifying.

Gina's medical training might have prepared her for a lot of things, but not this. Not industrial diving in a toxic environment with jury-rigged equipment and a countdown timer measuring lives in hours instead of days.

"You see anybody else?" Gina's voice carried a shadow of hysteria, the professional calm cracking to reveal the fear underneath. Her eyes were bright with unshed tears, but her jaw was set with determination that made her look older, harder. "Eight thousand people, Ketch. Eight thousand."

The number hung between them like a physical weight. Ketch could feel it in her chest, a crushing pressure that made it hard to breathe. Eight thousand souls, each one of them depending on decisions made by two people who were barely keeping themselves together.

Ketch wanted to scream at the dumb, waifish, selfless doll sitting in the copilot's chair. Wanted to shake her until some sense rattled loose, make her understand that heroic gestures only worked in entertainment vids where the physics were negotiable and nobody stayed dead. But she stopped herself, biting back the words that wanted to pour out.

Gina wasn't the only one on the brink of hysteria.

Ketch could feel it bubbling in her own throat. The taste of metal in her mouth, the way her vision seemed to narrow at the edges, the sudden certainty that everything was about to go catastrophically wrong.

Bad enough this ship was stuffed with corpsicles, sleeping passengers who looked too much like corpses in their transparent pods. But real corpses? If this went wrong, if they failed, she'd be flying a tomb. She'd carry the stink of rotten luck for years after this. Assuming she survived to tell the tale.

She was never, ever, ever going fly another corpsicle scow. The universe could find someone else to babysit the frozen families through asteroid fields and stellar debris. Someone with stronger nerves and a weaker imagination.

"I'll do it," Ketch said.

The words came out before she could stop them, before the rational part of her brain could catalog all the reasons why this was a terrible idea. She could have slapped herself for the impulse, but it was too late.

A host of arguments screamed into the front part of her brain, the supposedly thinking part that should have been running this conversation instead of her mouth. *You can't swim. You hate enclosed spaces. Water means death in space. Let the doc handle her own ship. Her own people. Her own disasters.*

But looking at Gina—really looking at her, taking in the exhaustion and determination and barely controlled fear—Ketch knew she couldn't let her do this. The woman was running on medical training and stubborn will, but that wouldn't be enough when she was underwater in a toxic pool trying to move equipment that weighed more than she did.

Gina tilted her head, auburn curls catching sparkles from the overhead lights, her brows raised in expectation. Waiting for Ketch to realize something, to connect dots that were apparently obvious to everyone except the person who'd just volunteered for a suicide mission.

What was she missing?

The silence stretched between them, filled only with the steady background noise of the ship—air recyclers working overtime, the soft percussion of debris impacts translated through the scanner array, the electronic chatter of navigation systems tracking their path through the asteroid field. Normal sounds that felt surreal in the context of their conversation, like discussing funeral arrangements at a birthday party.

"Would be dumb to save the people only to lose them to an asteroid breach," Gina finally said, her voice gentle but implacable.

Oh. That.

The asteroid cluster was still approaching, still demanding a pilot's attention and expertise. The navigation displays showed their projected path in cheerful blue and orange lines, intersecting with the ship's trajectory starting in exactly seventeen minutes.

Not a catastrophic collision, but close enough to require constant monitoring, careful application of the five little rock-splitting laser guns, split-second decisions if anything went wrong.

The doc had experience with scanners, maybe. She could cover the basic navigation functions for a few hours, keep the ship from drifting into anything immediately fatal. Point and click piloting for someone with medical training and steady hands.

Well, no. She couldn't. Not really.

Navigation through an asteroid field required instincts honed by years of experience, the ability to read trajectory plots and mass distributions and gravitational interactions in real-time. It required someone who could feel the ship's responses through the pilot's chair, who could anticipate problems before the computers recognized them. Who could hear the changes in the patter of rocks across the giant scow's hull. Medical training might teach you to read data, but it didn't teach you to fly.

But Ketch couldn't let her drown, either. Couldn't sit in this stupid chair watching the doc struggle alone in a brackish pool, fighting an environment that could kill her a dozen different ways. The thought made her stomach churn.

"Frankly, I'm the less jelly-legged option right now." Ketch heard the strain in her voice, tried to counteract it. She snapped her fingers. "Reflexes sharp."

It was true, as far as it went. Her body was fully

functional, her mind clear, her motor skills uncompromised by chemical fog and muscle atrophy. If someone had to make this dive, better the person who could actually coordinate her movements properly.

"All I need to do is fall down the water and help the bot clear the drain." Gina's reasonable tone was far better than Ketch's, carrying the calm authority that came with practice, medical training, and years of making life-or-death decisions. "And my suit is ready."

She gestured toward the hall, where her emergency equipment was presumably waiting in the med bay. Standard crew gear, designed for someone her size, properly fitted and maintained. Unlike Ketch's battered EVA suit with its mismatched gloves and jury-rigged repairs, Gina's equipment would be pristine, regulation-compliant, built to protect a ship's chief medical officer in whatever crisis might arise.

She was right. Somebody needed to do it—and now, not in a couple hours when the asteroid cluster passed and demanded every scrap of Ketch's attention. Who knew how long the repair would take— probably fifteen minutes just to get to the damn tank through the ship's maintenance corridors. Or thirty, for someone still shaky from hibernation, still learning how to trust her own balance.

The countdown timer caught her eye again: 3:37 and falling. Every second they spent arguing was another second lost, another step closer to the point where even a successful repair wouldn't matter.

The mathematics were simple and brutal. Fix the problem now, or watch eight thousand people suffocate in their sleep.

Ketch swallowed hard, tasting coppery fear. Her throat felt tight, constricted, as if the pool's toxic water was already filling her lungs. She needed to be in the action, needed to do something with her hands instead of sitting and watching disaster unfold on a screen.

But Gina was right. It was her ship, her people, her call. Medical training meant she understood the risks, knew exactly what they were asking her body to endure. If she thought she could handle it, if she was willing to take the chance…

The thought of letting her go alone still made Ketch's stomach clench. But the alternative—abandoning the navigation station during a critical approach, potentially killing them all anyway—was even worse.

"Fine," Ketch said. Nothing was fine about this. " But you keep your comms turned on." She touched her ear, feeling the familiar weight of the communications bud nestled against her skin. "And we turn on the mother computer's voice, too. Just in case."

CHAPTER
SEVEN

GINA FOUND her spacer suit where she'd left it, nestled in the white-paneled cupboards standing sentinel along the medical suite's walls. The familiar antiseptic smell of the room wrapped around her like a sterile embrace—ozone from the air purifiers, the faint chemical tang of sterilization compounds, the clean absence of human scent. Her hands trembled slightly as she opened the cabinet doors, the clear panels revealing neat rows of equipment arranged with near-military precision. Everything in its place, labeled and catalogued, a monument to the careful preparation that was supposed to keep everyone safe.

The suit hung there like an empty shell of herself, the gray and white composite material catching the soft overhead lighting. Medical grade, top of the line, with reinforced joints and enhanced mobility systems. She'd never worn it after the final fitting session, never expected to need it for anything more dangerous than a routine EVA inspection. The fabric felt strange under her fingertips—slightly rough, designed for durability rather than comfort, with the peculiar flexibility that came from materials engineered to remain supple in vacuum.

And, a little bit farther down the cupboards, the drawer with the stimulant drugs. That tomato soup was going to need a partner to keep her sharp underwater, to cut through the lingering fog of hibernation and the growing haze of exhaustion. The modafinil tablets were small and white, innocuous-looking things that could push human consciousness past its normal limits. Her medical training catalogued the risks automatically—increased heart rate, elevated blood pressure, the potential for cardiac arrhythmia in stressful situations. But the alternative was trying to perform complex underwater repairs while her brain was still swimming in chemical soup.

Her stomach wasn't ready for hard food yet, maybe because of the awakening process, maybe because of the nearly debilitating anxiety that made everything taste like metal and fear. The stimulant would have to be enough, artificial alertness layered over natural exhaustion like paint over rust.

She stepped into the suit—boots and all. The material enfolded her legs and torso with surprising warmth. The internal temperature regulation was already working, sensors detecting her body heat and adjusting accordingly.

It sealed itself around her with a soft hiss of equalizing pressure, the smart fabric contracting and expanding until it fit like a second skin. This was a new style, with extra pockets for medical equipment and very flexible gloves hidden under the protective over-mittens. The inner lining was soft against the skin of her neck, a mercy she hadn't expected.

As soon as she had slipped the separate dome of a helmet on, leaving it unlatched for the moment, the ship's computer started talking to her. The helmet was heavier than she'd expected, its weight settling on her shoulders like responsibility made manifest. The transparent aluminum visor was perfectly clear in front, offering an unobstructed view of the medical bay that suddenly seemed farther away, as if she were already separated from the world of air and warmth.

The suit's heads-up display came online as soon as the seals engaged, bathing her vision in soft blue readouts. Atmospheric pressure, oxygen levels, suit integrity—all nominal, all reassuring. For a moment she felt safer, protected, wrapped in technology designed to keep her alive in the most hostile environments humanity had ever encountered.

"Decontamination process ready." The ship's computer had a female-presenting voice that sounded like it had a second job guiding meditations. Calm, soothing, utterly inappropriate for the circumstances. There was something unsettling about the AI's tranquil tone when discussing procedures that could kill her.

"Thank you, ship," she said, her voice echoing strangely inside the helmet. The acoustics were different here, her words bouncing back with a slight delay that made her hyperaware of her own breathing. As she clunked across the gray-rubber floor over to the cradle she'd just left—an hour ago? Two? Time had become elastic, unreliable—she glanced at the window overlooking Cradle Room One.

All those people. Thousands of transparent pods stretching into the distance, each one containing a dreaming soul who trusted her to keep them safe. Families who'd sold everything for passage to a new world, children who would never see their new home if she failed. The weight of their unconscious trust pressed down on her like the helmet's physical weight, making it hard to breathe.

She quickly looked away, focusing on the medical equipment around her instead of the sleeping multitude. "Hey ship, can I call you *Autumn Dream*? Or just *Dream*?"

"That's fine, doctor." The AI's response was immediate, accommodating, as if giving comfort to dying crew members was just another function programmed into its behavioral matrix.

"Gina is fine." She seemed to remember telling the system that earlier, though the hibernation drugs made her memories feel unreliable, like trying to recall a dream. Maybe it thought she'd forgotten, the way people sometimes did after trauma or chemical intervention.

Gina stood beside her empty cradle, its padded arms now folded closed like a creature sleeping while it waited for its next occupant. The similarity to a coffin was impossible to ignore—the way it lay there, patient and ready, designed to hold a human body in perfect preservation. She shuddered, the movement constrained by the suit's bulk.

"Ketch?" she asked, needing the sound of another human voice to cut through the medical bay's sterile silence.

"Copy, Doc. Looking good from Nav. Standing by." Ketch's voice was warm in her earpiece, carrying undertones of concern wrapped in professional competence. The connection felt like a lifeline, proof that she wasn't completely alone in this antiseptic wilderness.

She positioned herself over the wide square drain on the floor next to her cradle, where her sleep-soup had disappeared earlier in what felt like another lifetime. The metal grating was solid beneath her boots, and she thought she could hear the faint echo of water flowing somewhere far below. Above her, the ceiling opened with a mechanical purr that seemed to fill the entire medical bay, reverberating off the peach-colored walls and walls and boxy medical equipment.

First, a monster shower head descended from the hidden recess, its surface gleaming with the promise of chemical cleansing. Then a circle opened up around it with the precision of surgical instruments, revealing the decontamination chamber's true scope. A clear plasticky cylinder dropped slowly, inch by inch, until it touched the floor around her with a soft pneumatic sigh. The material was transparent but distorting, making the medical bay beyond look like something seen underwater.

She felt like a specimen being collected, trapped in a glass cage while unseen forces prepared to transform her into something fit for preservation. The comparison made her skin crawl beneath the suit's protective layers.

The air in the helmet tasted of antiseptic and new plastic, with a hint of cinnamon. Had she been chewing gum during the fitting? The helmet's full weight settled on her shoulders as six mechanical seals engaged from neck to collar with decisive clicks. Like the cradle's seals, but in reverse. Boxing her up again, separating her from the world of breathable air and human touch.

She wasn't ready to be re-boxed, wasn't ready to be sealed away from life and warmth. The hibernation had been enough imprisonment for several lifetimes.

But eight thousand people were counting on her, and the countdown timer in her peripheral vision showed two hours, forty minutes remaining.

"Ready," she said anyway, though the crack in her voice echoed inside the helmet like a confession of fear.

The first flood of decontamination liquid cascaded

from the shower head with the force of a waterfall. The sound was deafening inside the cylinder, a drumming roar that seemed to penetrate even the helmet's automatic sound dampening. It came down more forcefully than necessary, just like her "relief water" had during the awakening process—as if the ship's systems were designed by people who believed that more pressure meant better results.

But this time, instead of panic and gasping, Gina stood firm, wide-legged, against the chemical onslaught. She watched the thick, oily fluid sluice down her suit like liquid mercury, carrying invisible threats away in streams of silver-gray. The decontamination mixture smelled like industrial solvent and medical-grade bleach, she knew from experience. Smelled like nothing, here in her suit. Her suit's external sensors registered the chemical composition —compounds that would strip organic matter down to its component molecules, leaving only sterile polymer and metal behind.

The liquid stopped with a sudden silence that felt almost violent after the roar of the shower. A second spray began half a minute later. A fine mist that clung to the suit like frost had clung to the cradles in the hibernation rooms. The droplets were perfectly uniform, each one a tiny lens that caught and scattered the overhead lighting. The mist gradually thickened into a shellac that hardened quickly under the hot air of the dryer cycle, creating a secondary barrier between her and the toxic environment she was about to enter.

Droplets beaded and slid down her visor like shining stars, each one carrying away another microscopic threat.

Two hours, twenty-five minutes. The numbers floated in her peripheral vision like a death sentence, counting down with relentless precision.

"Doing great, doc." Ketch's voice surprised her, cutting through the mechanical sounds of the decontamination cycle like a warm hand on cold metal. "Yeah, I can see you. Computer says she'll let me watch you as you go. *Dream* and I, we're friends now." She chuckled, a sound that rumbled through the comm system with genuine warmth. "Crisis friends, at least."

The idea of Ketch watching over her was unexpectedly comforting. Someone who cared, someone who would know if things went wrong. Someone who would remember her if she didn't make it back.

When the cycle finished, the cylinder released from the ceiling with a soft hiss of equalizing pressure. The top and bottom sections closed automatically, forming a loose bubble around her that moved with the same liquid grace as the hibernation fluid. The material was nearly invisible, more felt than seen, like being wrapped in solidified air.

Gina took her first step, and the protective barrier moved with her like a ghostly dance partner. The sensation was surreal—being enclosed but mobile, protected but isolated. Her boots thudded against the flooring with each step, the sound muffled by the barrier but still audible. The rhythm was steady, determined, the sound of someone walking toward danger because there was no other choice.

Gina turned down the hall the other way. She thudded past two openings in the wall with ladders leading down into darkness. Past maintenance alcoves filled with equipment she couldn't identify. The corridor felt different now, more ominous, as if the ship itself were holding its breath. Emergency lighting cast harsh shadows that seemed to move independently, creating the illusion of movement where there should be none.

The elevators at mid-ship waited with mechanical patience. The sliding doors of the nearest elevator were already open, revealing an interior that looked like a vertical tomb—gray walls, harsh lighting, just large enough for a person and their big protective bubble.

She stepped inside, feeling the elevator's systems engage with a subtle vibration that traveled up through her boots.

The descent felt endless, though it probably lasted less than a minute. Through the elevator's small port-hole, she caught glimpses of the ship's interior structure—massive support beams, the complex network of pipes and conduits that kept eight thousand people alive, the industrial architecture that was usually hidden behind clean walls and pleasant lighting.

The ship was a vessel on its last cruise. At Gliese, once all the people were safe on the planet. *Autumn Dream* would be broken up for parts and pieces to build the first towns. The computer would take on a new life as environmental controls and security for the first settlements.

On the lower floor, only one hallway was lit. *Dream* taking no chances with medicos with no sense of navigation. The corridor stretched ahead like a tunnel, its walls lined with warning signs and emergency equipment. As Gina walked down the hall, her boots made the same tap dance rhythm on the metal-rubber flooring that they had when she'd walked the rows of sleepers during her final inspection. Her stride was pretty much the same speed, too, thanks to the modafinil now coursing through her system.

The stimulant was working, sharpening her focus and steadying her movements, but she could feel its pressure on the system. Her heart rate was elevated but controlled, her mind clear but somehow disconnected from her body's fatigue. It was like being a passenger in her own nervous system, watching herself perform with chemical-enhanced precision.

What looked like regular hall walls here were actually the first layer of the eight giant pools' containment systems. The deception was complete—nothing to suggest that beyond these innocent-looking surfaces lay industrial tanks filled with toxic liquid and sleeping machinery. When Gina stepped through the only open door, her bubble trailing like a second shadow, she saw the wall was as thick as her forearm. Solid metal, designed to contain pressures and chemicals that could kill in seconds.

After she passed through, she heard the hiss as *Dream* slid the door shut behind her. She turned to see a second door drop from the top of the inner edge of the doorway she'd come in, sealing her into an airlock between the ship's living spaces and its industrial heart. The sound was decisive, final. No chance of contamination in either direction.

Ten steps on, another door, another thick wall. Each barrier was a reminder of how dangerous this environment was, how many safeguards had been built to keep people away from the liquid breathing systems, the liquid cryo systems, the liquid fuel.

And here she was, about to dive into the very heart of what all these protections were designed to prevent.

"Still with me?" she said over the comms.

She heard a pop of connection, and then Ketch breathing—steady, controlled, the sound of someone trying to project calm. "Always. Didn't want to distract you."

The simple presence of another person's breath in her ear eased her heart. So warm, so necessary.

"You're not," Gina said. "You can stay on." After she passed through the second thick wall, she watched the first and second doors slide down with the same precision and finality as at the first wall. The airlock systems were working perfectly, sealing each section as she passed through like a series of one-way valves. "I want you to."

The words came out more vulnerable than she'd intended, but they were true. The connection to Ketch felt like her last link to the world of air and warmth, to the possibility of survival. Of life.

The last, inner wall was thick metal, its surface scarred by decades of maintenance and repair. The door was a fancy oval with a wheel in the middle to open it—industrial design that prioritized function over form, built to withstand pressures and corrosive chemicals that would destroy conventional materials.

"I'm at the porthole," she said, though porthole seemed like too soft a word for the utilitarian hatch that stood between her and the toxic pool beyond.

"The hatch?" Ketch's voice carried a note of tension, carefully controlled. "How do you feel?"

Two hours, seven minutes. Relentless, that countdown. Marking time until disaster with all the indifference of the universe.

"Super." The lie tasted metallic in her mouth, mixing with the suit's weird cinnamon air.

"Liar," Ketch said, and Gina could feel the smile in her voice. "I see your mittens shaking."

The observation was accurate. Her hands were trembling inside the suit's gloves, fine tremors that spoke of adrenaline and suppressed fear. The video feed was apparently good enough to catch details she'd hoped to hide.

"Video's bad," she protested weakly.

"So go on then, spin the wheel." Ketch's voice carried forced cheer, the kind of artificial encouragement people used when they were trying to convince themselves as much as others.

"Wait," said *Dream* in its ethereal way. "Contraction commencing."

The bubble around Gina ripped in the front with a sound like tearing fabric. The material somehow extended and floated its edges to the pool wall, flowing like liquid while maintaining its structural integrity. The process was unsettling to watch, as if the laws of physics were negotiable when it came to the ship's more exotic technologies.

"What even is that stuff?" Ketch asked, voicing the question that was echoing in Gina's mind.

"Tricomposite micromolecule self-adhesing maintenance gel," *Dream* replied with the kind of technical precision that was utterly unhelpful for actual understanding.

"Needs a nickname," Ketch said with forced lightness. "Call it…cellophane."

"What's that?" Gina asked. The word was unfamiliar, though it had a pleasant sound—soft and translucent, like something that might wrap gifts rather than protect people from industrial toxins.

"One of my mom's favorite words. She's all about the dead languages." There was a catch in Ketch's voice when she mentioned her mother.

The bubble sealed itself to the circular wall with a

whoosh-pop that seemed to echo through Gina's bones. She was committed now.

"Push the buttons to the right of the door wheel," Dream instructed with meditation-leader calm. Four mechanical push buttons lined up with the axle of the wheel on that side, each one worn smooth by countless cycles of maintenance and emergency procedures. "This is the order: One, three, two, four."

Two clanks echoed through the protective barrier as internal mechanisms engaged. A slot opened toward the bottom of the door, revealing the first glimpse of the pool beyond—dark water that reflected the harsh industrial lighting like black glass.

"Lame code," Ketch commented, the lightness in her voice not quite masking her worry.

Welcome to the club.

"You didn't know it," *Dream* replied with unshakeable tranquility, apparently programmed to defend its security protocols even in casual conversation.

"Hey!" Gina yelped as the liquid air began to fill the space around her, surging up from the opened slot with surprising force. It rose past her knees, her waist, her chest, pushing hard against her protective barrier. The liquid was cold even through the insulation. But the smell didn't reach her. Probably a blessing—she'd been breathing this liquid until just today. What if she'd caught the scent and just fallen right asleep again?

Gina fought for balance as the artificial

atmosphere tried to knock her off her feet, the thick fluid creating turbulence that made standing upright a constant struggle. For a moment, she forgot the helmet, forgot the protective barriers between her and the toxic environment. Instinct took over, and she took a deep breath and held it, her body responding to the sight of rising liquid with panic reflexes honed by millions of years of evolution.

Then she exhaled slowly, forcing herself to remember the technology keeping her alive.

"Submersion complete," she said, her voice somewhat steady. Of course it would be as cold here as in a sleeper's cradle.

Gina spun the wheel lock, feeling the mechanism turn with surprising smoothness despite its ancient appearance. The door clicked and swung open away from her, revealing the pool's interior in all its terrifying glory. Dark water stretched away into shadows, with that bigger shadow of the dead maintenance bot wedged against the drain like a sleeping monster.

She hesitated at the threshold, her body's survival instincts screaming warnings that her rational mind had to override. Every evolutionary impulse told her to flee, to seek air and warmth and safety. But eight thousand people were counting on her, and the countdown timer showed Two hours, one minute, ticking.

"Get going," Ketch said, her voice carrying conviction that Gina desperately wanted to believe.

"Two hours remaining," said *Dream* with its

maddening calm, as if announcing the time until breakfast rather than disaster.

Gina stepped through the threshold into the dark water. The liquid closed over her helmet with the finality of a closing coffin lid.

She began her descent into the industrial heart of humanity's ark.

CHAPTER
EIGHT

KETCH COULD ONLY WATCH as Gina let herself fall forward into the viscous liquid, and the helplessness of it made the pilot want to punch something. Her hands gripped the edge of the console until her knuckles went white, the textured metal surface biting into her palms. The navigation center suddenly felt like a cage—all this sophisticated equipment, all these controls at her fingertips, and none of it could help the small figure disappearing into the deep below.

The pool was huge, much larger than the schematic had suggested. The computer—*Dream*, what a pretentious name for a ship stuffed with sleeping people—had given Ketch two camera views: a wide shot from somewhere near the top of the pool that made everything look distant and unreal, and the one they already had, the spider bot's view down by the blocked vent. But the lighting was absolute crap, harsh industrial floods that created more shadows than illumination, turning the liquid into an alien ocean where anything could be lurking.

The wide view reminded Ketch of surveillance footage from prison cells or morgues—clinical, remote, reducing a human being to a moving dot on a screen. She hated it immediately, hated the way it made Gina look small and expendable, just another piece of equipment being deployed to solve a technical problem.

Gina was dropping from what looked like the center of the pool, in terms of height. The suit's lights shone bright around her helmet, smaller navigation strobes dotted her arms, sides, and legs like a constellation of desperate stars. She was all spread out, arms and legs extended like someone sky diving, but not going anywhere fast through the thick, viscous medium. The liquid seemed to grab at her, holding her back with invisible hands.

From above she looked like a shiny bug caught in black amber, suspended and struggling against forces too large to comprehend. The image made Ketch's stomach clench with sympathetic claustrophobia. She'd always hated enclosed spaces, always preferred the vast emptiness of space to the cramped confines of ship corridors and sealed chambers. But this was worse—Gina was trapped in liquid darkness, surrounded by chemical soup that would crush her in seconds if her suit failed.

Then Gina did something at her waist—probably

adjusting the ballast controls—and started to sink faster. The movement was deliberate, practiced, the kind of technical competence that came from good training. Ketch felt a flicker of hope. Maybe the doc knew what she was doing after all.

Ketch leaned closer to the display, her face almost touching the screen, fingers hovering uselessly over the navigation controls that were suddenly irrelevant. The familiar rhythm of asteroid tracking and trajectory plotting seemed meaningless when someone might be drowning somewhere in the bowels of the ship. Some dream.

The air in the navigation center tasted stale, like it couldn't keep up with Ketch's too-fast breaths. Her tank top clung to her back, stuck by dried perspiration that had nothing to do with the room's temperature.

"Heart rate elevated, doctor," *Dream* announced with that maddening meditative calm. "One hundred forty-seven beats per minute."

The AI's voice grated on Ketch's nerves like sandpaper on skin. Computer better not be broadcasting Gina's vital signs to anyone else, better not be treating this like just another medical procedure to be documented and filed away. The clinical detachment in *Dream's* tone made Ketch want to grab the nearest tool and start smashing things until the ship showed some real emotion.

"Hey, doc," Ketch said, forcing her voice to sound

casual despite the tension knotting her shoulders. "How you doing?"

A long pause filled only with the sound of Gina's rapid breathing through the communications system, each inhale and exhale amplified and distorted by the suit's microphones. The breathing was too fast, too shallow, the kind of hyperventilation that preceded panic attacks and poor decisions. Ketch found herself unconsciously matching the rhythm, her own chest rising and falling in sympathy.

"Cold," Gina finally managed, her voice small and distant. "Really cold."

Of course she was cold. The pool was kept at hibernation temperatures, the same bone-deep chill that those eight thousand Sleeping Beauties. Ketch watched as Gina's arms and legs moved in stilted, awkward motions through the viscous medium. The resistance of the liquid seemed to be fighting her every effort, turning simple movements into exhausting struggles against an environment that wanted her dead.

The thermal readouts on Ketch's secondary screen painted a grim picture in false colors—Gina's core temperature dropping steadily while her extremities blazed warning yellow as the suit's heating systems fought a losing battle against the industrial cold. The numbers were clinical, precise, and absolutely terrifying.

"Keep going," Ketch said, trying to inject confidence into her voice while her own heart hammered against her ribs. "You're doing great."

A lie. Gina was struggling, fighting the liquid and her own exhaustion and the chemical fog that still clouded her thinking. But what else could Ketch say? That she looked like she was drowning? That the thermal readings suggested hypothermia was at the door? That an entire ship's load of people were going to die because they'd asked too much of someone who'd been awake for less than three hours?

"My thoughts are..." Gina's voice trailed off, the words slurring slightly. "Going fuzzy."

Even with the stimulants? Had anybody ever tested giving a person modafinil hours after they woke up from twelve years of chemical hibernation? After an emergency "hot" re-entry that should have taken days instead of hours? When they had to perform underwater repairs in an environment that could kill them in dozens of different ways?

Yeah, right. They were flying blind, making it up as they went along, hoping that human stubbornness and medical training would be enough to overcome impossible circumstances.

"Breathe, doc. Just breathe. You know how." She hoped Gina wasn't as oppositional-defiant as everybody said Ketch herself was. The doc better listen, better trust the voice in her ear, because there was nothing else between her and disaster.

"One hour, fifty-one minutes," *Dream* interjected with its eternal serenity.

"Thanks so, so much," Ketch muttered. The AI was probably too stupid to recognize sarcasm. "Super helpful." The countdown timer felt like slow-water torture, each announcement a reminder of how little time they had left, how many things could still go wrong.

On the screen, Gina had stopped moving entirely, floating suspended in the dark liquid like a frog in formaldehyde. Ketch shivered. They were about to lose her. The suit's lights created a small sphere of illumination in the darkness, but beyond that bubble lay an ocean of industrial night that could swallow her without a trace.

"Doc?" Ketch's voice rose, cracking with strain she couldn't quite hide. "Gina? What's happening?"

The silence stretched like a held breath, filled only with the background hum of ship systems and the distant percussion of asteroid impacts against the hull. Each second felt like an hour, each heartbeat like thunder in the confined space of the navigation center.

"I can't—" Gina's voice thin like breaking glass. "I can't do this. Can't breathe."

Ketch could hear the panic building in her voice, could recognize the signs of someone approaching complete breakdown. She'd heard that tone before, in her own voice during her worst moments, when the universe felt too big and hostile to survive. The sound made her chest tighten with sympathy and terror.

"Your suit is working great," Ketch said, glancing

at the readouts that confirmed what she was saying. "Perfectly. *Dream* says better than expected. Oxygen-nitrogen levels steady. It just feels tight because you're anxious."

The lie came easily, born from years of emergency situations where calm confidence was more important than absolute truth. The suit was working, but Gina was dying by degrees—hypothermia, exhaustion, chemical interference with her already compromised nervous system. But acknowledging that wouldn't help anyone.

"No, no, no," Gina's words tumbled out in a rush, panic bleeding through the comm system like poison. "It's like waking up again. The fluid in my lungs. I'm drowning."

Hibernation trauma. Of course. Ketch should have anticipated this, should have realized that being surrounded by liquid would trigger memories of the awakening process. Gina had spent twelve years breathing fluid, then violently expelled it during emergency revival, and now she was surrounded by more liquid in an environment that looked disturbingly similar to a hibernation pod.

"Absolutely not," Ketch said firmly, putting every ounce of authority she could muster into her voice. "This is different. Way different. You're safe in your suit. So safe."

But Gina wasn't listening. Her breathing had accelerated to rapid, shallow gasps that echoed through the comms. On the thermal readout, her core temperature was dropping while her extremities were already flashing warning colors that meant frostbite and nerve damage. The suit's heating systems were losing the battle against the industrial cold.

"Heart rate one hundred eighty-two," *Dream* declared. "Recommend administration of sedative."

Ketch wanted to reach through the screen and strangle the AI's virtual neck. "Can we even do that?" she snapped.

A pause that felt like eternity. "No," *Dream* admitted, maddeningly calm.

Of course not. The doc was sealed in her suit, isolated in a freezing pool, surrounded by liquid that would kill her if even a single seal failed. There was no way to administer drugs, no way to provide physical comfort, no way to do anything except talk her through the crisis and hope it was enough.

"Gina, listen!" Ketch's voice cut through the comm static with desperate urgency. "You need to move. Arms and legs."

"Yes," *Dream* agreed in its therapeutic tone. "Excess activity will warm you up and keep you alert."

No response. Just rapid, shallow breathing that suggested complete panic. On the screen, Gina floated motionless in the dark water, her suit lights creating a small island of illumination in the industrial ocean. She looked like a dying star, fading against the black.

"Temperature in lower extremities approaching critical threshold," *Dream* said.

Ketch closed her eyes for a moment, forcing herself to think past the panic and terror. The navigation center's familiar sounds—the hum of life support, the electronic chatter of tracking systems, the distant percussion of debris impacts—all of it faded into background noise as she focused on the problem at hand.

What would help? What would reach through the panic and hibernation trauma and chemical confusion to connect with the person drowning in fear below?

"Hey, Gina," she said softly, changing tactics completely. "Tell me about Gliese."

A fast inhale through the comm, sharp and desperate. A pause filled with the electronic whisper of suit systems and life support.

"What?" Gina's voice was small, confused, like someone waking from a nightmare.

"Do you have a spot picked out? When you get there?" Ketch kept her voice gentle, conversational, as if they were sitting in a quiet café instead of managing a crisis that could kill eight thousand people.

"I..." Another pause, longer this time. "There's a lake," Gina said hesitantly, the panic starting to recede from her voice.

"Tell me about it," Ketch said, leaning forward in her chair until she was almost touching the screen. "What does it look like?"

As Gina began to describe the green-blue water and the palm trees surrounding her imagined paradise, her breathing gradually slowed. The words came haltingly at first, then with growing confidence as she found refuge in dreams of warmth and sunlight. On screen, her limbs started to move again, making snow angels in the dark liquid as muscle memory and determination overcame panic.

The sight made Ketch's chest tight with relief and something else—pride, maybe, or admiration for someone who could find hope in the middle of a nightmare. Gina was describing a world she might never see, painting pictures of beaches and sunshine while floating in industrial poison, and somehow that was enough to keep her moving.

"Good," Ketch said, her voice rough with emotions she couldn't quite name. "Tell me more."

"We're supposed to be able to swim in it," Gina continued, her voice steadier now, growing stronger with each word. "Can you believe it? Actual swimming, not just…this."

"One hour, forty-two minutes," Dream interjected with its eternal serenity.

Ketch ignored the computer, focusing instead on the miracle happening on her screen. Gina was moving again, sinking deeper into the pool with deliberate strokes. "Looks like you're two-thirds there. Little bit more."

The wide-angle view showed Gina's slow progress downward. Each movement was a victory against physics and chemistry and her own body's desire to give up. She was almost at the edge of the spider bot's light when she suddenly stopped again, floating motionless in the dark water.

"So tired," she said, her words slurring slightly. Hypothermia and exhaustion catching up to her. "Gonna rest a minute."

Alarm bells squalled in Ketch's mind. She threw herself back into her chair, grabbing handfuls of hair, tugging at them.

"Absolutely not!" she snapped, abandoning any pretense of calm. "It's the cold, affecting your thinking. Keep moving, keep warm."

"Like I'm back in the cradle," Gina murmured, her voice taking on the dreamy quality. "This is just a…"

"Gina? Gina!"

"A big cradle, right? Just…sleep for a while…"

The girl had been sleeping until just hours ago. Sleeping for twelve years in chemical suspension, her body and mind preserved in artificial hibernation. Her body probably thought sleeping was her natural state, that consciousness was the aberration. In her current condition—hypothermic, exhausted, drugged with stimulants and confused by hibernation aftereffects—the urge to return to that peaceful darkness must be almost irresistible.

"*Dream*," Ketch said, her voice tight with control. "Cut her out a minute."

"Pilot Ketch, I have shifted you to a different channel." The AI's response was immediate, efficient, serene.

"Gina can't hear us?"

"Correct."

The navigation center felt suddenly empty without Gina's breathing in Ketch's ear, without the connection that had been their only link. Ketch stared at the screen where the small figure floated, so still, in the dark water.

"What happens if she goes to sleep down there?"

"Everyone dies." *Dream's* response was matter-of-fact, delivered with the same tone it might use to announce the weather.

Literal-minded computer. "No, I mean, she sleeps ten minutes. Like she did up here. Would that help her? Reset her system?"

"Ten minutes of no movement would not be advisable." The AI's therapeutic tone made Ketch want to scream.

Shit. Of course not. Ten minutes without moving in that environment would mean hypothermia, possible coma, probably death. And even if Gina survived, she'd wake up even more confused and disoriented than before.

"Okay," Ketch said through gritted teeth.

"It might not kill her—" *Dream* continued with maddening precision.

"Okay, I said."

"—But it might damage important limbs needed to effectuate the repair."

"Okay!" Ketch slammed her hand on the console, the impact sharp and satisfying against her palm. "How about we get Gina back in the stream?"

The comm channel shifted with an electronic pop, and suddenly Gina's voice was back—slurred, distant, already half-asleep.

"Easier to get going after a short reset...rest...resting..."

"No!" Ketch was still riled up, her voice sharper than she'd intended. The word came out like a gunshot in the confined space of the navigation center. "No sleeping!"

"Yeah, just a minute...or two..." Gina's voice was fading, consciousness slipping away like water through her fingers.

"Gina!" Ketch slammed her hand on the console again, putting all her frustration and fear into the gesture. The impact sent vibrations through the metal structure, through her bones, a physical reminder that she was here, solid, real, while Gina drifted in chemical limbo below. "The spider bot can see you now. You're close to the bottom. Look down."

On the spider cam view, Gina had come into frame like a descending angel—all white and gray in her protective suit, moving like a dead leaf in water. The dormant maintenance bot was still slammed against the vent, unchanged since they'd first spotted it, a massive obstacle that might as well have been a mountain for all the hope Ketch had of moving it remotely.

"See it," Gina said, her voice distant. "The blockage."

"Go to it," Ketch urged, leaning forward until her

forehead almost touched the screen. "You're so close now. Just a little bit farther."

With visible effort, Gina propelled herself downward the final distance through the thick fluid. Her movements were clumsy, exhausted, but determined. Each stroke was a victory against the forces trying to stop her—the cold, the chemicals, her own body's desire to surrender to the peaceful darkness of unconsciousness.

Her boots touched the bottom of the pool with a soft impact that Ketch felt in her chest like the tap of a small hammer.

"I made it," Gina said, sounding surprised by her own success. "I'm here."

Ketch blew out a breath she didn't realize she'd been holding, the tension leaving her shoulders in a rush that made her feel suddenly boneless. She reached for the cabinet under the console with shaking hands, needing something to ground herself, something normal and routine. Time for a drink, even if it was only water.

Gina had made it to the bottom, reached the blockage that threatened everything. All that was left was just mechanics—moving the bot, clearing the drain, saving everyone.

The hard part was over.

CHAPTER
NINE

"GREAT JOB," Ketch said, her voice tight and buzzing through the comm system like she had been the one to take the modafinil. The sound seemed to come from very far away, distorted by the liquid medium and her helmet's speakers. "Now move toward the vent."

Gina's limbs felt distant, disconnected from her brain's commands, as if she were operating a marionette with tangled strings. The liquid around her wasn't really water—it was heavier, denser, pressing against her suit from every direction with the weight of industrial purpose. Each movement sent ripples through the viscous medium that seemed to move in slow motion, hypnotic and strange.

Her thoughts moved at the same sluggish pace, as if the thick fluid had somehow entered her head as well, replacing her brain with the same chemical soup that had filled her lungs during hibernation.

The modafinil was losing its battle against exhaustion and hypothermia, its artificial alertness overwhelmed by the demands of her compromised nervous system. She could feel it wearing off in waves, each surge of fatigue deeper than the last, like a tide that kept rising higher on the beach of her consciousness.

"One hour, thirty-one minutes," *Dream's* voice floated in her helmet, serene and detached as always, the AI's meditation-leader calm utterly inappropriate for the circumstances.

One and a half hours until everyone died. The thought should have terrified Gina, should have sent adrenaline surging through her system to override the crushing fatigue. But instead it seemed abstract, academic, like a problem from a textbook rather than immediate reality. Somebody would read about them in a medical journal someday, with distant, clinical interest. Or maybe an engineering manual. Case study in system failure and human limitations.

"Gina! Move toward the vent." Ketch's voice cut through her detachment with sharp urgency. "It's right there."

Okay, fine. The words formed in her mind but took work to translate into action. Everything required such effort now—thinking, moving, even breathing seemed to demand more energy than she had to give.

Gina took a slow step through the industrial soup. This liquid was so much heavier than water, thick and clinging, so she didn't bounce with each movement the way she would in a swimming pool. Or maybe it was the weights clipped to her belt, designed to keep her from floating up to the surface like a cork. Either way, each step felt deliberate, measured, as if she were walking on the ocean floor rather than the bottom of a maintenance tank.

The pool floor was eerily smooth beneath her gloved boots, like walking on black glass that had been polished to perfection. No debris, no texture, just the unnatural smoothness of industrial engineering designed to be cleaned and maintained by machines rather than humans. The lights from her helmet cast strange, elongated triangles that danced and shifted with each movement, creating patterns that seemed almost alive in the dark water.

She couldn't hear the liquid around her—no splash or gurgle, just the muffled sound of her own breathing inside the helmet. Each exhale fogged the visor slightly before the suit's climate control cleared it away, a rhythmic cycle that had become hypnotic. It felt like she was moving through a dream, where the normal rules of physics and sensation didn't quite apply.

The silence outside was profound, oppressive. Sealed in her suit, with just her breathing, her heartbeat, and the occasional electronic chirp from her suit's systems, the isolation was complete, absolute. Like being buried alive in chemical amber.

"Do you see the bots?" Ketch broke into her thoughts, her voice a lifeline to the world above.

"Yes," Gina managed, though her tongue felt thick in her mouth, clumsy and unresponsive. The word came out slurred, barely recognizable. "Big."

The blockage was worse than it had looked on the monitors. Much worse. What they'd seen through the cameras was just shadow and suggestion. The reality was intimidating in a way that video couldn't capture. The maintenance bot's torso was basically a metal box as big as a draft horse, wedged tightly against the vent opening as if it had been sucked there by a powerful vacuum. The surface was scarred and pitted from years of industrial use, covered in warning labels and access panels that spoke of complex internal machinery.

Five of its six articulated limbs splayed out toward her like a giant metallic shrimp, each one as thick as her waist and ending in specialized tools she couldn't identify. Welding equipment, maybe, or cutting torches. One limb had actually penetrated the grating of the vent, disappearing into the dark opening like a tentacle reaching for prey. The sight made her stomach clench with claustrophobic dread.

"It's stuck," she said, the words requiring enormous effort to form. "Right up by the wall."

The spider bot chose that moment to swim-run up to her, its remaining legs churning through the liquid air with mechanical enthusiasm. Its headlight blazed directly into her face, flooding her visor with harsh white light that made her eyes water and sent spikes of pain through her already aching head.

"Cut it out!" Gina floated a mittened hand up to shade her eyes, the movement slow and awkward. The bot's light was designed for industrial work, not human comfort—too bright, too focused, like staring into a welder's torch.

The spider bot retreated, but only to the floor where it settled beside her knee with what looked almost like embarrassment. It appeared lopsided and sort of tragic with its missing legs and sliced-off rear, like a wounded animal trying to be helpful despite its disabilities. At least it seemed happy to see her, its remaining lights blinking in what might have been a greeting.

She should sit down for a moment. Take a rest. Just for a minute.

The spider bot scuttled back to the maintenance bot. So small! How had they ever thought this bot could move that hulk of a maintenance bot.

Gina started to bend her knees. She could sit right down, here. Nothing said she couldn't.

"Doctor," *Dream* said, so calm. "The golden hour is passing."

Golden hour. The term punched her in the solar plexus. Brought back memories of trauma bays and emergency rooms, where that phrase meant the differ-ence between life and death. Get the patient stable in the first hour after injury, and you had a good chance of a positive outcome. Miss that window, and the statistics turned grim very quickly.

Gina's years of training kicked in despite the fog clouding her thoughts, a distant voice of reason cutting through the exhaustion and chemical interference. The emergency protocols were still there, buried under layers of fatigue. Assess the situation. Identify the problem. Formulate a plan. Execute with precision and speed.

She needed to focus. Eight thousand lives depended on her clearing this vent—eight thousand souls including her medical team, the people who should have been here to help her, who would never wake up if she failed. The weight of their trust pressed down on her like the liquid around her suit, making every movement harder, every breath more labored.

Too much responsibility. Too much pressure. "I need to…" Her voice trailed off as she struggled to complete the thought, her mind losing track of what she'd been trying to say. The words seemed to dissolve before they could reach her tongue, like sugar in water.

"Gina?" Ketch's voice wouldn't let her drift away, wouldn't let her sink into the comfortable fog of exhaustion. Ketch could handle anything, it seemed—asteroid fields, uncooperative computers, panicking doctors.

An idea formed slowly in her sluggish mind, a way to make the impossible weight of responsibility more manageable. "Ketch? Could you hold onto eight thousand souls for me? I need my hands free."

The request sounded absurd even as she said it, but it felt necessary somehow. She couldn't carry all that responsibility alone, not in her current state. If Ketch could take some of the weight, maybe she could function well enough to complete the repairs.

A pause that stretched like eternity.

"You got it," Ketch said finally. "Sure thing. I'll babysit your sleepers, doc. Don't you worry."

So. Time to assess the problem with professional detachment, the way she'd been trained to approach medical emergencies. Remove emotion, focus on facts, develop a treatment plan.

The spider bot seemed to have the same idea. It scuttled toward the trapped maintenance bot with renewed purpose, wriggling into the narrow space between the massive machine and the pool wall. The gap looked impossibly small, but the bot squeezed through with the fluid grace of something designed for exactly this kind of work. Once positioned, it lifted two of its remaining legs and tapped the side of the metal box with mechanical precision.

Push. The message was clear, unmistakable.

Dream must have figured out a solution, developed a plan using the resources available. So now Gina could skip straight to the execution phase, no need for complex analysis or creative problem-solving. Just follow the plan. Pray it worked.

The knee-high spider bot made the positioning

look effortless. But it was a tight squeeze to get a human body into that same cramped space. The gap between the maintenance bot and the wall was barely wide enough for her shoulders, and the angle was awkward, requiring her to contort her body in ways the suit wasn't designed for.

Gina held her breath—more from habit than necessity—and led with her hip, scootching into the space with careful deliberation. The maintenance bot rocked slightly as she pressed against it, its massive bulk shifting just enough to give her maybe another inch of working room. The movement sent vibrations through the liquid that she felt more than heard, a low-frequency rumble that seemed to come from the machine's internal systems.

So the bot wasn't dead, just sleeping. Offline, for some reason.

Waiting for help.

Wedged between the wall and the bot, her back pressed against cold metal and her hands tucked up against her chest, Gina realized this wasn't the optimal angle for applying force. The position was cramped, uncomfortable, putting all the mechanical disadvantage on her side. She felt like she was trying to move a mountain with a teaspoon.

Her first attempt yielded nothing, just the frustrated strain of muscles working with no purchase against an immovable object. The maintenance bot was jammed tight, held in place by physics and bad luck and probably a dozen other factors she couldn't identify. Stupid thing might as well have been welded to that grate in the the floor for all the good her pushing was doing.

The spider bot positioned itself against the wall next to Gina and lined up all six of its remaining legs against the maintenance bot's hull. Together, they pushed—woman and machine working in awkward partnership against the laws of physics. Gina groaned with the effort, the sound echoing inside her helmet like a prayer or a curse.

The massive box shifted, just the slightest bit. Barely perceptible, but enough to prove that movement was possible. Enough to give her hope that this might actually work.

The small success also gave her a better angle, better leverage for the next attempt. She could brace her arms more effectively now, use her body's natural mechanics instead of fighting against them. The positioning was still awkward, but workable.

First, though, she had to catch her breath. The effort had taken more out of her than it should have, leaving her gasping inside the helmet like she'd just run a marathon. A wave of dizziness washed over her, making the dark water seem to spin around her in lazy circles. The lights on her helmet seemed to dim, then brighten, then dim again, as if her suit's power systems were struggling to keep up with demand.

Her eyelids felt like they were turned to sand, heavy and gritty, demanding to close despite her desperate need to stay alert. The hypothermia was winning, shutting down her body's systems one by one in preparation for the big sleep.

"Gina!" Ketch's voice jolted her back to awareness like a slap across the face. "Stay awake!"

She shook her head violently, fighting against the fog that wanted to claim her consciousness. The motion sent waves through the liquid around her, disturbing the perfect stillness of the industrial pool. The dizziness receded slightly, pushed back by willpower and the adrenaline surge that came with recognizing how close she'd come to losing the fight.

"Listen," Ketch said, her voice cutting through the chemical haze with sharp urgency. "I think you have enough space now."

"For what?" The question came out slurred, barely intelligible.

"Get your feet up, doc. Use your legs. Kick the bastard off."

The suggestion made sense from a biomechanical standpoint—leg muscles were stronger than arms, could generate more force with better leverage. "Better," Gina agreed, though the thought of contorting her body into even more complicated positions was exhausting.

"Exactly. Can you get your foot up against the bot?"

Getting into position required pulling her knee up while twisting to the right, a maneuver that the suit's joints barely allowed. The fabric stretched and creaked with the movement, servo motors whining as they tried to assist her motion. Her cold muscles added their protests to the symphony of discomfort already playing in her head—cramps and spasms and the deep ache that came from working in an environment her body wasn't designed for.

Every muscle in her body, already strained from the cold and exhaustion, protested the awkward positioning.

"Should have taken more yoga classes," she groaned, pushing the words out between labored breaths.

"I see you," Ketch said, and there was warmth in her voice despite the circumstances. "Doing great."

Once the first leg was set, braced against the maintenance bot's body, the second one was easier to position. Not easy—nothing about this was easy—but at least she had a sense of what movements the suit would allow and what would leave her trapped in an impossible position.

"Feel like a spider bot," she said, looking across at her boots with something that might have been humor if she hadn't been so tired.

"You look like a spider bot," Ketch said, and Gina could hear the smile in her voice despite everything. "Now act like one. Push!"

Gina pushed with everything she had left, her legs screaming with the effort. The maintenance bot's hull was slick under her boots, offering minimal traction, but she found purchase on some kind of access panel and used it as a foothold. The machine groaned and shifted, fighting against whatever forces held it in place.

"Keep pushing!" Ketch yelled, her voice sharp through the automatic sound dampeners in Gina's headset.

Gina yelled back—not words, just sound, a primal expression of effort and determination that echoed inside her helmet like a war cry. The maintenance bot shifted slightly under the combined pressure, then more, its massive bulk finally overcoming whatever had held it trapped.

Then suddenly it broke free with a rush of movement that sent shockwaves through the thick liquid. The bot drifted sideways away from the vent opening, no longer a lifeless obstacle but a functioning machine again. It collected itself quickly, pulling its splayed limbs together and regaining its balance like a cat landing on its feet. One limb remained behind, still stuck in the grate.

Almost immediately, Gina felt a current tug at her suit as liquid began flowing through the newly cleared opening. The movement was subtle but unmistakable—the system was working again, circulation restored, the crisis beginning to resolve itself. She pushed off from the wall and away from the vent, giving the machinery room to do its job.

"One hour, twenty-three minutes," *Dream* said.

Less than half an hour had passed since she'd entered the pool? It felt like hours, like she'd been fighting in this toxic environment for most of her life. Time had become elastic, unreliable, measured by heartbeats and exhausted breaths.

The spider bot tugged at the jammed leg, slowly working it free from the grate. Then it hop-scuttled, carrying the limb to the maintenance bot.

"You did it!" Ketch's voice held a note of triumph that Gina couldn't quite share. The repair was complete, the immediate crisis resolved, but she was too tired to feel anything resembling victory.

Her knees buckled without warning, and she found herself kneeling on the smooth pool floor like a supplicant before an altar. The sensation was oddly comforting despite the circumstances, like sinking into a soft bed after the longest day of her life. The liquid around her felt less hostile now. Kind of like a warm bath.

"What are you doing?" Ketch demanded, her voice sharp with alarm. "Gina, get up!"

"Resting," she murmured, the word coming out slow and thick. "Just a minute." Just long enough to gather her strength, to let her body recover from the impossible demands she'd placed on it. Surely she'd earned that much.

"No resting!" Would Ketch ever stop shouting? The woman's voice cut through the peaceful fog like a knife, dragging Gina back toward consciousness when all she wanted was to drift away into the comfortable darkness. "You have to get back to the hatch. It's too cold to sleep down there."

Gina knew Ketch was right—the logical part of her brain, the doctor and scientist trained to recognize the signs of hypothermia and oxygen deprivation, understood the danger perfectly. But that voice was growing fainter, drowned out by the siren song of sleep, promising an end to cold and pain and impossible responsibility.

The spider bot suddenly darted in front of her face, its bright light and round body blocking her view of the seductive darkness ahead. One of its legs tapped against her visor with sharp insistence, a metallic ping that echoed inside her helmet like an alarm clock she couldn't turn off.

"Go 'way," she mumbled, weakly batting at the persistent machine with one mittened hand. The movement was uncoordinated, clumsy, like trying to swat a fly while wearing oven mitts.

Her eyelids drooped. Just a moment's rest, that's all she needed. A brief respite from the cold and the pressure and the weight of eight thousand lives depending on her success. Then she would find the ladder—there had to be a ladder somewhere in this. She would climb back up, through the hatch and back into the protective bubble, pass through the thick walls, return to the world of air and warmth and human touch.

After a bit. After she'd recovered enough strength to make the journey.

Something large and heavy shoved her from the side, knocking her sideways onto her backside with enough force to send ripples through the viscous liquid. Gina forced her eyes open, blinking away the fog of exhaustion. The horse-sized maintenance bot, now apparently fully functional and mobile, had positioned itself on one side of her. The little spider bot remained on the other, like mechanical bookends keeping her from falling over completely.

"Doctor Johnson," *Dream* said, "the maintenance bot would prefer that you leave. Humans are an unnecessary pollutant in the pools."

The AI's tone was as serene as ever, but the message was clear. Gina was no longer welcome in this sterile environment. Her job was done, her presence an contamination that the ship's systems wanted removed as quickly as possible.

"So much for gratitude," Ketch said, and there was something that might have been laughter in her voice.

Gina let out a long sigh that fogged her visor briefly before the climate control cleared it away. She didn't want to stay where she was unwanted, didn't want to be just another piece of debris cluttering up the ship's perfectly ordered systems.

"Understood." She placed her hands on the pool floor, feeling the slick surface through her thick gloves as she pushed herself up. Her body felt impossibly heavy, as if gravity had doubled or tripled while she'd been kneeling. Every muscle screamed in protest.

She shut the door on their screams and kept pushing. Kept fighting the weight and the exhaustion and the voice in her head that whispered how much easier it would be to just lie down and let everything go.

The ladder to the hatch seemed impossibly far away, an endless journey across the smooth floor of an alien ocean. It couldn't actually be that far, but distance was relative when every step required enormous effort, when the thick liquid fought her movement and her own body betrayed her.

Trick of the water, she told herself. Optical illusion caused by the refractive properties of the industrial fluid and the inadequate lighting. The ladder was closer than it looked, the journey shorter than it seemed.

She hoped.

One step at a time, the way she'd learned to handle every impossible challenge in her life. Just like medical school, when the workload seemed insurmountable and every day brought new crises that threatened to break her. Just like residency, with its endless hours and life-or-death decisions that no amount of training could fully prepare her for. Just like qualifying for this once-in-a-lifetime adventure, this journey to a new world that had seemed like a dream when she'd first applied.

One foot in front of the other. One breath after another. One heartbeat following the last until she reached safety or died trying.

She took a shambling step forward, then another, her movements uncoordinated but determined. The spider bot moved ahead of her through the thick liquid, leading the way like a tiny mechanical guide dog. Its little lights blinked in what might have been encouragement, or maybe just the random firing of damaged circuits.

She wasn't moving fast enough for the maintenance bot, apparently. The massive machine bumped her again, this time from behind, its bulk lifting her up in the water with surprising gentleness. Before she could protest or lose her balance, it slid underneath her like a mechanical whale offering a ride to shore.

"Hold on," *Dream* said, its calm voice carrying what might have been amusement.

The maintenance bot waited until Gina had wrapped both arms around its metal carapace, then rocketed toward the ladder and then all the way up with the speed and precision of a machine that had found its purpose. The journey that would have taken her precious minutes to complete on foot was over in the time it took to draw a single breath.

"Woah," said Ketch.

As soon as Gina's hand reached for the hatch wheel, the maintenance bot was gone, vanishing back into the dark water with the same efficiency it had shown in rescuing her. Luckily, there was a small ledge on this side of the hatch where she could stand while working the manual controls, a concession to the possibility that humans might occasionally need to access this area.

She heard the beautiful click of mechanical locks disengaging as the wheel turned, followed by the hiss of equalizing pressure. The sound was like music—the promise of escape from this toxic environment, of return to the world of air and warmth. She tugged on the wheel, using her body weight to help swing the heavy hatch open.

As the hatch swung out, opening into the pool, it pushed her off the ledge. She grabbed for the wheel, her mittened hands slipping on the wet metal, and missed. The current from the opening pulled at her, threatening to drag her back into the dark water.

She still had the ballast weights clipped to her belt, the extra mass that had helped her sink to the bottom but now threatened to drag her down when she needed to rise. The maintenance bot was going to be seriously miffed if she polluted its clean pool by drowning in it.

But the spider bot hadn't abandoned her. The little machine scurried to the top of the open hatch and extended two of its remaining legs toward her like mechanical lifelines. Gina managed to grab hold of one leg, and the bot pulled her back toward the ledge with surprising strength.

She thought she heard it chirping at her through the liquid medium, a sound like electronic birdsong that might have been encouragement. Or it might have been her oxygen-deprived brain interpreting random mechanical noises as communication.

Gina pulled herself through the opening with the last of her strength, collapsing onto her hands and knees on the corridor floor. The protective bubble surrounding the door flexed and adapted to her presence, maintaining its seal despite the sudden intrusion. The spider bot followed her through, then turned to pull the heavy hatch closed and spin the wheel back to its locked position.

Gina rolled to a seat on the floor. As the liquid from the pool drained out of the safety bubble, the little bot floated down to settle in her lap like a mechanical cat seeking warmth. Its lights blinked in slow, steady patterns that reminded her of stars—distant, beautiful, and utterly peaceful.

The floor beneath her was blessedly solid, blessedly still after the fluid environment of the pool. No current, no resistance, just the familiar firmness of deck plating warmed by the ship's heating systems. Her eyelids drooped once more, heavier than they'd ever been, demanding the rest her body so desperately needed.

Her last conscious thought was of the spider bot settling deeper into her lap, its damaged form somehow comforting in its determination to help. Its lights continued to blink like distant stars, like the navigation beacons that guided ships safely home through the darkness of space.

Like hope, persistent and bright against the endless night.

THE ELEVATOR DESCENDED TOO DAMN slow.

Ketch had given it thirty minutes after clearing the asteroid cluster—enough time to navigate the *Dream* through the last of the floating debris, enough time for the adrenaline to fade from her system, enough time for Gina to wake up on her own and call in with a cheerful "all clear" that would ease the knot of worry that had taken up residence in her chest.

But the comms had remained silent, leaving nothing but the familiar background symphony of ship operations—air recyclers humming their mechanical lullaby, the distant percussion of pebble impacts against the hull, the electronic whisper of systems caring for eight thousand sleeping souls.

The silence felt wrong, ominous in a way that made her fingers twitch toward controls that couldn't help. The next asteroid field had required her full attention, demanding split-second decisions and constant monitoring, but now that they were through the worst of it, the worry came flooding back like water through a broken seal.

"*Dream*, how's our Doc doing?" Ketch asked, drumming her fingers against the elevator wall. The metal was cool under her fingertips, vibrating slightly with the car's descent through the ship's super-structure.

"Doctor Johnson's vital signs are stable but subdued. She appears to be in a deep sleep state." The AI's voice carried its usual meditation-leader calm, but Ketch was learning to read the subtle variations in its tone. This sounded like carefully controlled concern wrapped in clinical detachment.

Ketch had expected that answer, but it still made her stomach tighten. Stable was good, but subdued could mean anything from normal recovery sleep to hypothermic coma. And deep sleep after severe hypothermia wasn't always the peaceful rest it appeared to be. Sometimes it was the body's last desperate attempt to conserve resources before systems began shutting down permanently.

"And the temperature in that corridor?" she asked, though she already suspected the answer would be bad news.

"Nineteen degrees Celsius. Within acceptable parameters, but cooler than optimal for recovery from hypothermia."

Nineteen degrees. Cold enough to keep someone

from warming up properly, cold enough to prevent the kind of recovery that Gina desperately needed. The ship's heating systems weren't designed to accommodate humans in the industrial sections—those areas were meant for maintenance bots and emergency repairs, not for people to spend extended periods recovering from near-death experiences.

The elevator doors finally slid open with a pneumatic sigh, revealing a corridor that felt like stepping into a walk-in refrigerator. Ketch broke into a jog, her boots echoing down the empty hallway with sharp, metallic impacts that seemed to bounce off the walls and multiply into a percussion symphony of urgency. The sound was wrong here—too hollow, too isolated from the warm, lived-in spaces above. The air tasted thin and sharp, like freezer burn and machine oil.

The corridor felt different from the upper levels—more utilitarian, more obviously part of the ship's mechanical infrastructure. The walls were thicker, designed to contain pressures and temperatures that would be lethal to human life. Emergency lighting cast harsh shadows that moved strangely as she ran, creating the illusion of movement where there should be none.

When she reached the airlock sequence, she kicked into high gear. She'd seen this as Gina passed through. Through the first thick barrier, across the decontamination space, through the second wall designed to keep the toxic environment contained. Each seal hissed shut behind her with mechanical finality, marking her passage deeper into the ship's industrial heart.

She saw the protective bubble—that weird "cellophane" stuff, tricomposite micromolecule whatever—still intact around the hatch like a transparent cocoon. The material shimmered slightly in the harsh lighting, its surface rippling with subtle distortions that made the space inside look underwater.

And there, curled on her side like a sleeping child, lay Gina.

The sight hit Ketch with a tornado of emotions. Relief that Gina was there, was breathing, was apparently intact. Fear at how small—how fragile—she looked inside the protective suit, how utterly still she lay on the cold deck plating. And something else—something that felt suspiciously like tenderness, an unfamiliar warmth that had nothing to do with the corridor's industrial chill.

The spider bot perched on Gina's hip like a mechanical guardian, its remaining legs positioned protectively over her torso. The little machine's lights blinked in slow, steady patterns that somehow conveyed watchfulness, dedication, a determination to protect the human who had helped it complete its mission. At Ketch's approach, it raised two legs in what looked oddly like a greeting—or maybe a warning not to disturb its charge.

The gesture was so unexpectedly human that Ketch found herself smiling despite her worry. The bot had clearly appointed itself as Gina's protector, taking its role seriously with the kind of single-minded dedication that only machines could manage.

The bubble parted for her as she approached—*Dream's* doing, no doubt. The material flowed away from her like liquid silk, creating an opening large enough for her to enter while maintaining its seal against the entrance to the liquid-oxygen pool.

Ketch knelt beside Gina on the deck plating, feeling the cold seep through her knees despite the ship's heating systems. Through the helmet she could see the toll the underwater repair had taken. Gina's face was pale, almost translucent, with faint blue shadows under her eyes and around her lips that spoke of oxygen deprivation and severe cold exposure. But her chest rose and fell in steady rhythm, and her suit's readouts showed normal life support function.

"Doc? Hey, Doc?" Ketch placed a hand on Gina's shoulder, the suit's material rough on her hand as she gave it a gentle shake. The fabric was slightly stiff from the decontamination process—that weird coating—but she could feel the warmth of the human body beneath.

Nothing. No response, no flicker of consciousness, just the steady breathing that meant her body was still fighting to recover.

"She requires warmth," *Dream* said, eternally calm. "And proper medical attention."

No shit.

"Give me a hand here, spider," Ketch muttered,

sliding her arms under Gina's shoulders and knees. The suit made her heavier than she looked, its protective layers and life support systems adding bulk and weight to the small frame beneath. But Ketch had handled cargo and equipment in all kinds of conditions. This was just another problem requiring careful handling and determined effort.

The small bot scuttled away from Gina's hip, its lights blinking in what might have been acknowledgment or confusion. So much for mechanical assistance. Apparently, the spider bot's protective instincts didn't extend to helping with actual rescue operations.

Dream had said to leave the suit on until they reached the medical bay—something about maintaining stable temperature and avoiding rapid pressure changes that could trigger additional medical complications. The AI's guidance made sense from a clinical standpoint, but it meant carrying Gina's unconscious form through the ship's corridors while she remained sealed inside her awkward protective cocoon.

Ketch managed to lift her with a combination of leverage and stubbornness, and draping Gina over her shoulder in a fireman's carry that distributed the weight more evenly. The position wasn't particularly dignified, but it was stable and allowed her to navigate the narrow corridors without risking a fall that could injure them both.

By the time she reached the main corridor,

breathing hard from the effort and the stress, a cargo bot had appeared—a flat bed transport with short railings that hovered at waist height. The little spider bot was perched on top like a hitchhiker, its little running lights blinking brightly.

"Thanks, Spider," Ketch said. She carefully rolled Gina onto her back on the cargo platform. The bot's mechanisms adjusted automatically to accommodate the new load. No soft padding, but at least it was flat.

The journey to the medical bay felt endless, though it probably took less than ten minutes. Ketch walked alongside the transport, one hand resting on Gina's shoulder through the suit, monitoring her breathing and vital signs as best she could without proper medical equipment. The spider bot remained at its post at her feet, a pint-sized sentinel keeping watch over its human companion.

Twelve hours later, according to *Dream's* precise chronometer, the doc was still asleep.

Ketch had managed a few hours of restless cat-napping in the medical bay's recovery rooms, called in the required status report to Deacon Base—"all's well, no problems, proceeding on schedule"—without mentioning the near-disaster or the unconscious woman currently occupying the chief medical officer's private quarters.

Now Ketch was back in the navigation center, casually monitoring their progress through the tail end of the asteroid field. The familiar routine of checking trajectories and adjusting course felt surreal after the intensity of the crisis, like returning to normal life after a particularly vivid dream. She was listening to the gentle percussion of pocket asteroids pinging against *Dream's* hull, a soothing rhythm that had become her constant companion during the long weeks of solitary navigation.

"How're the rocks?" a voice asked from behind her.

This time, Ketch managed not to jump out of her skin, though her heart rate spiked with surprise and something that felt suspiciously like joy. She swiveled in her chair to look at Doc Gina, drinking in the sight of her. Conscious and upright and apparently functional.

Same bland medical-issue tights that somehow looked elegant on her small frame, but she'd traded the oversized marshmallow sweater for a new jewel-green tunic that brought out the color of her eyes. The yellow headband had been replaced with something in wild raspberry that made her auburn curls look like they were on fire. No ugly sweater in sight—apparently, the near-death experience had improved her fashion sense.

Most importantly, her eyes were clear and sharp, focused with the kind of alert intelligence that meant her brain was fully online and functioning normally. The hypothermic fog had lifted, leaving behind someone who looked rested, recovered, and ready to take on whatever challenges the universe might throw at them.

"Just coasting along," Ketch said, trying to keep her voice casual despite the relief flooding through her. The asteroid field was cooperating, their trajectory was stable, and the woman who'd saved eight thousand lives was standing in the navigation center looking like she could take on the world.

Gina lifted her arms into a V for victory, and Ketch noticed she had a drink bulb in each hand. The gesture was playful, triumphant, utterly at odds with the serious medical officer who'd volunteered for a suicide mission less than twenty-four hours ago. "Ginger ale," she announced with obvious satisfaction. "All the liquor's locked deep in the hold with the rest of the luxury supplies."

"Works for me," Ketch said, accepting the offered bulb with fingers that were steadier than she'd expected. The ginger ale was cold and sharp, with the artificial zing that marked it as ship-standard refreshment rather than anything approaching the real thing. But it did taste like celebration, like shared relief and the simple pleasure of being alive to complain about synthetic flavoring.

Gina sank into the co-pilot's seat with obvious pleasure, smiling as the padding molded itself to fit her petite frame. The chair had been designed for larger people, but it seemed to welcome her now, adjusting its contours to provide proper support for someone who'd earned the right to sit in the place of honor.

"All this advanced technology," she said with

mock complaint, "and my feet still don't touch the floor."

The observation was so perfectly ordinary, so wonderfully mundane after everything they'd been through, that Ketch found herself grinning.

"Just one of the many reasons this boat was sent out on a one-way mission," she said. Cheap construction, minimal comfort features, designed by people who never expected to ride in it themselves."

Gina lifted her bulb in a toast, extending it toward Ketch with ceremonial gravity. "To surviving ships built by the lowest bidder."

Ketch leaned closer to "clink" their bulbs together, a gesture that felt both silly and profound. As she moved, she caught Gina's scent—less like the industrial freezer burn of the lower decks and more like flowers now. Warm sunshine-meadow flowers, with undertones of the medical bay's clean antiseptic and something uniquely human that spoke of life and recovery and stubborn determination.

Damn, she smelled better than antifreeze and OJ. Gotten used to the silence, hadn't she?

"Can't figure out why my legs are still so wobbly," Gina said after taking a sip of her ginger ale, rolling her ankles experimentally. "Stiff, like I ran a marathon in concrete boots."

"Well," Ketch said, settling back in her pilot's chair with the satisfaction of someone delivering a particularly effective reality check, "you did push a five-hundred-pound maintenance bot with your legs.

While hypothermic. After being asleep for twelve years. In a crevasse of a pool that wasn't designed for human occupation."

A small smile tugged at Gina's lips, transforming her face from merely pretty to genuinely beautiful. "Put it that way, it sounds almost impressive."

"It was impressive," Ketch said firmly, meaning every word. "It was goddamn heroic. You saved eight thousand people today. Well, yesterday."

"Don't see that every day." She shrugged. "Saved the whole damn popsicle parade, you did."

"We did," Gina corrected, looking directly at Ketch with an intensity that made her stomach flutter with unfamiliar warmth. "Couldn't have done it without you talking me through the panic, keeping me focused when I wanted to give up."

Ketch's cheeks went hot. She looked away, focusing on the familiar displays and readouts that suddenly seemed less important than they had moments before. "You did the hard part. All I did was sit in a comfortable chair and offer moral support."

The spider bot chose that moment to click-clack into the navigation center. It now sported all its original appendages in apparently perfect working order, and moved with the confident gait of a machine that had found its purpose. Which was, apparently, carrying two of the premium protein bars in its manipulator claws like an offering to honored guests.

Ketch reached down and accepted the bars, noting their superior packaging and gourmet labeling.

"Chocolate caramel delight," she read aloud. "Well, look who's been promoted to VIP status."

"New friend?" Gina asked, accepting the bar Ketch offered her with obvious amusement.

"Not the only one," Ketch said, waving at the six main monitors that now displayed comprehensive ship status information she'd never had access to before. "Guess who's ship boss now? *Dream* finally decided I'm family. About time. Even spilled where you lot hide the decent snacks." She bit off a chunk of chocolate caramel delight, savoring flavors that were a significant upgrade from her usual standard rations.

The chocolate was real—or at least a convincing synthetic approximation—with layers of flavor. The caramel was smooth and sweet, coating her tongue with the kind of luxury she'd almost forgotten existed.

They let the quiet linger, comfortable in each other's presence in a way that felt both new and ancient. The navigation center seemed smaller some- how, more intimate, as if the crisis had transformed it from a workspace into something approaching a home. Flowery scent wasn't such a bad change from the usual mixture of recycled air and industrial lubri- cants that characterized most ship environments.

The doc sure did dress like a flower, all bright colors and soft textures that somehow managed to look both professional and approachable. What even was the color of that headband? Chartreuse? Magenta? Something that existed in nature but didn't have a proper name, like the color of tropical sunsets or exotic fruit that grew on worlds she'd never seen.

"So what happens now?" Ketch finally asked, though part of her was afraid of the answer. The crisis was over, the immediate danger past, and that meant a return to normal procedures—whatever normal meant for a ship carrying eight thousand sleeping colonists toward a distant star.

"Not sure," Gina said, her expression growing thoughtful as she gazed over the monitors toward the windows that revealed the endless expanse of space beyond. "I thought I should start the proper revival protocol for Chen and Diallo. They're the chief engineers—they could help make sure nothing like this happens again, implement better safeguards, redundant systems."

She paused, taking another sip of ginger ale, and Ketch could see the weight of responsibility settling back on her shoulders like a familiar but unwelcome coat. "But *Dream* says it's not necessary now. The maintenance bots have identified and fixed the root cause of the problem. The automated systems are back online and functioning well."

Another pause, longer this time, filled with the soft electronic chatter of ship systems and the distant percussion of debris impacts against the hull.

"And I don't want to put anybody else through the emergency revival process for nothing," she said. "It's traumatic, disorienting. Chen and Diallo don't deserve to go through that unless there's a genuine emergency requiring their expertise."

She sighed, a sound that carried the exhaustion of someone who'd been making life-or-death decisions for too long. "So...it's back to sleep for me, I guess. Until we reach Gliese in four years."

The chocolate on Ketch's tongue turned to cardboard. Of course. Gina would go back into hibernation—that was the plan, the whole point of the colonist ships. People slept through the journey and woke up at their destination, ready to start new lives on a distant world.

But the idea of watching Gina disappear back into chemical sleep, of having to return to the solitary existence Ketch had grown accustomed to during her weeks aboard the *Dream*, felt suddenly unbearable. Not just lonely. Actively painful, like the prospect of losing something precious she'd only just discovered.

"Right," she said, trying to keep her voice neutral despite the turmoil in her chest. "Of course. That makes sense."

"Will you..." Gina paused. "Would you help me get back into my cradle when the time comes? It's silly, but after what happened with the pool and the liquid breathing, I'm a little..."

"Traumatized by the idea of going back in a liquid coffin?" Ketch supplied, understanding immediately. Anyone would be hesitant to return to hibernation after nearly drowning in a pool of the stuff, after experiencing the panic and disorientation of emergency revival.

Gina grimaced at the blunt phrasing, but nodded. "I was going to say 'anxious,' but yes. The thought of being surrounded by fluid again, of trusting my life to automated systems that have already failed once…"

Ketch swallowed hard, the request tasting like obligation and loss and something that might have been broccoli if broccoli could break your heart. "Of course," she said, meaning it despite the way the words seemed to stick in her throat. "Whenever you're ready. No rush."

She turned to gaze out into space, where the asteroid field continued its ancient dance around distant stars. Four more weeks of piloting the *Dream* through the remaining debris, four more weeks of navigating by instruments and instinct through a maze of rock and ice that could kill them all if she made a single mistake.

"Got another month of piloting through this field," she said, trying to sound matter-of-fact. "I wasn't lonely before—got used to my own company, actually preferred it most of the time. But now…"

She glanced at Gina, taking in the bright colors and soft curves and the way her presence made the navigation center feel like a place where people actually lived rather than just worked. "Place'll seem emptier, now. Didn't mind it before. Might now."

Something flickered in Gina's eyes—surprise, maybe, or recognition of something she'd been thinking herself. The expression was there and gone too quickly to interpret, but it left Ketch with the feeling that she wasn't the only one dreading the return to solitary existence.

"What if I stay up?" Gina asked suddenly, the words tumbling out as if she'd been holding them back and finally lost the battle with herself. "Until you have to leave, I mean. Until your contract ends and you transfer back to your own ship."

Ketch felt her heart stop, then resume beating at roughly twice its normal rate. "You mean, not go back in the cradle right away? Stay conscious for weeks?"

"I'm already awake," Gina said, her voice gaining confidence as she spoke. "And I've checked the supply inventories. We have enough food, water, and life support consumables for one additional person to stay conscious for months if necessary. The margins are built in for exactly this kind of situation."

She hesitated, looking down at her hands where they rested on the chair's armrests. "And I…I'm not ready to go back under. Not yet. The thought of being unconscious, helpless, trusting my life to systems I can't monitor or control…"

Ketch felt something odd bloom in her chest, something warm and light and absolutely terrifying in its intensity. The possibility of company, of human connection, of sharing the navigation center with someone who understood both the beauty and the danger of space travel. The prospect of conversation, shared meals, the simple pleasure of not being alone with eight thousand sleeping strangers.

"Well," she said, trying to keep her voice casual despite the way her heart hammered against her ribs, "that would be all right with me. I mean, if you're sure you want to spend four weeks in a tin can with someone you barely know."

Gina laughed, the sound soft and warm and utterly delighted. "I think I know you well enough. Anyone who can talk someone through a panic attack while navigating an asteroid field and coordinate an underwater rescue operation is probably decent company."

"All right, then," Ketch said, and couldn't quite suppress the smile that wanted to take over her entire face.

Outside the windows, stars glittered against the infinite black like scattered diamonds on velvet. Asteroids tumbled in their bulbous orbits, following gravitational laws older than any civilization. Planets moved through their cycles in distant systems, carrying the promise of new worlds and fresh beginnings.

Somewhere among them was Gliese, Gina's ultimate destination, the blue-green world that eight thousand twenty-two people had sacrificed everything to reach. A place of lakes and forests and breathable air, where humanity could start over and build something better than what they'd left behind.

Might be worth trying to see it, one day.

ALSO BY NICKY PENTTILA

Cosmic Weave

Cooperative Realm: Frankie's Journeys

Cargo Trouble

Frankie Takes a Holiday

Frankie Takes a Dive

Frankie Finds a Dot

Frankie Takes a Bow

Cargo & Chaos: Frankie books 1 & 2

Cooperative Realm: The Arkhide Chronicles

Hidden Planet

The Listeners

The Elders of Arkhide

Tales of Arkhide story collection

Historical Fiction

A Note of Scandal

An Untitled Lady

The Spanish Patriot

ABOUT THE AUTHOR

Nicky Penttila wrote her first story, a Mayan murder mystery, in seventh grade. But then came gymnastics, math team, and boyfriends. Later came husband, car payments, and a sleep-depriving work schedule at newspapers across the country. Then came a second career as a science writer. But the fiction kept trickling out, a story here, a novella there, and finally, a real live novel. And she hasn't stopped.

Find more great reads at nickypenttila.com